T0104055

Lady with a Badge

Sandy Takes Over P.I., Inc.
Detective Agency

(This is a sequel to previous novel "P.I., inc.")

Patrick Ireland hands the reins of his Private
Detective Agency over to Sandy and she becomes
Miami's premier female private investigator.

Ken Bumpus

Trafford
PUBLISHING®   www.trafford.com
North America & international
toll-free: 1 888 232 4444 (USA & Canada)
fax: 812 355 4082

DEDICATED TO:

All the men and women in the US Armed Forces
and the 'men in blue" who protect and serve us'

K.

PROLOGUE

In the previous book ('P.I., inc.') Patrick Ireland was one of Chicago's best detectives until he was seriously wounded while trying to end a war among rival juvenile gangs. Put on permanent disability he retires to Miami and buys into a Private Detective agency.

Along with acquiring extensive computer facilities, designed by the previous owner, Andy Jackson (a 'Geek' among Geeks') he also inherited Andy's 'right hand man' Alejandra Maria Sanchez de Torrez (Sandy). She proved such an asset in the detective agency that, after six years, Detective Ireland turned over the reins of P.I., inc., Investigative Agency to her and went to being the security officer for the condominium where he lives.

This is <u>her</u> story

ONE

Miami was slowly drying out after a weekend onslaught of rain and wind brought on by an off-shore "Tropical Disturbance". The storm left behind very little real damage only a few downed trees (which were old and rotting) and the gutters clogged with leaves, plastic bags and fast-food wrappers.

Sandy was glad to see the blue sky and fluffy white clouds which greeted her on her way to the offices of **P.I., inc.,** Monday morning.

In the six months since accepting Patrick Ireland's offer of taking command of the detective agency, Sandy had successfully closed numerous background checks of on-line dating participants, and a couple missing persons cases, mostly routine investigating tasks.

She unlocked the door and stepped into the outer office. Her first objective, after entering the main room, was to make a quick check of the e-mails crowding her computer screen 75% of them were "Spam" and junk. She browsed through the others categorizing them into a semblance of priorities.

One message was from the agency's frequent client, Attorney Endicott

He was asking for a 'sit down' to discuss what he termed 'an extremely touchy case'.

This one Sandy put on the top of her list, and immediately picked up the phone to call the lawyer and arrange a meet.

"Hi, Counselor," Sandy greeted him, "Long time no-see. Watcha' got for me?"

"Hi, yourself, Beautiful. I'm afraid this one is too 'hush-hush' to discuss over the phone, so what about coming over to my office this afternoon and I'll lay it all out for you?"

"Fine, I'll see you about 1:30 then, OK?"

"Great. See you then."

At exactly 1:30 Sandy walked into Lawyer Endicott's office and was immediately usher into the attorney's private conference room.

"Sandy, this situation is going to call for some 'deep-cover' work on your agency's handling," he began, "My client is a VERY HIGH profile state official who can't afford to have this 'leaked' out. It could mean a real 'shake-up' in the state capitol if it became public!"

"WOW!" Sandy. Remarked, "You can depend on **P.I. inc.** to handle it with utmost discretion, Counselor."

"Fine. That's just as I expected. Now here's the deal My client is being 'blackmailed' by a young 'lady-of-the-evening' who claims to have incriminating pictures of him in very compromising situations. He claims the pictures are not of him but 'Photoshoped' ™ pictures with his head placed on someone else's body.!"

"Counselor, I think we can nip this in the bud real quick like. With the computer programs Andy left to us it should be a 'snap' to disclose the 'Photoshop' doctoring. Andy is a computer 'whiz' and has written software that will blow this Broads' case out of the water in a click of the mouse!"

"The incriminating photos are on a CD not prints and. . . . . ."

"HEY, Counselor, that's even better! With the CD I'll be able to examine the <u>pixels</u> that make up the images and I'll be able to determine which ones have been altered and just how!"

"Sandy, If you can squelch this one, you'll be able to write your own ticket in the state. of Florida!"

"All I need from you, Counselor is the CD and we can put this little 'Bitch' away for good."

"I can have the CD over to your office this afternoon!" Lawyer Endicott assured Sandy. "Gal, THANK GOD and Andy for technology!"

"Well, that one was easier than I expected," Sandy thought to herself as she drove back to the office.

Sandy immediately began doing her computer 'magic' and had completed the task by quitting time.

Early next morning she walked into Attorney Endicott's office with her results in hand.

"Nailed it, Counselor! Here's the blackmailer's CD and on this other CD I've mapped out click by click, the steps taken to unlock how the photos were 'doctored'!" Sandy proudly announced.

"Sweety, You did good!" he chuckled, "Now, all we have to do is set up a 'sting' to nail her with the goods!"

"I've been in touch with a couple of my CIs (Confidential Informants) in Miami's shady side, Sir, and they report that the gal behind this s . . .t is too dumb to be the 'master-mind' of the operation. Someone else is pulling her strings. It might surprise you to know, they say they believe the real crooks are two low-level members of a leftist Political Action Committee trying to 'rig' the next election. the money is just a cover-up."

"Damn! I should have seen the political ramifications this whole stinking case held," the Attorney cursed

The next thing Sandy and the Attorney decided to do was set up a 'pay-off sting' and round up the whole gang then they could call the case 'closed'.

"I've a plan it worked in a similar 'ransom' case Andy pulled off a few years ago, it could work again," Sandy suggested, "We'll package a GPS tracking device in the money bundle Andy designed the perfect instrument, and he left three of them in his deal with Patrick.

"They're wafer-thin and only about the size of two postage stamps easy to hide inside the bills and remotely controlled so we can turn it on and off at will to fool a scanner."

"Sounds great to me, Girl," Endicott agreed.

The blackmail victim contacted the woman and a meet was arranged.

He was instructed to go to the UPS office at 247 SW 8TH Street in the Brickell neighborhood. There he'd pick up a package addressed to him. In the package was a cel phone and a GPS tracking device. This device is secure so he could not track it without a password.

The money was to be packed in a cheap brown briefcase He was told he would receive instructions over the cel phone.

"Follow them explicitly! No tricks or COPS!"

The victim picked up the package and waited for instructions. Five minutes passed then ten minutes no instructions. Then the phone crackled to life and a voice (obviously distorted) told him to proceed south on I-95 to the first exit. Turn west and stop at the Chevron station and wait.

Following those instructions, he pulled into the parking lot, turned off the motor and waited. No sign of anyone who looked the least bit suspicious.

Meanwhile Sandy and her local policeman friends took up a position on a side street a block away to watch and wait.

Sandy feared that the crooks had been tipped, but, just as she was to call off the surveillance, a black sedan pulled alongside the victim's car and the voice on the cel phone snapped:

"Don't look around! just toss the briefcase in the back seat and get out of here!"

The victim quickly complied and sped off to the north, putting distance between the black sedan and his vehicle.

Sandy and her cops hesitated for a brief time so as not to arouse suspicion then carefully moved out in pursuit, keeping a good distance behind the black sedan. Sandy actually let the vehicle get out of sight. With her remote control tracker she periodically activated it to check the position of the felons, then switched it off to forestall them having time to discover it's signal.

The 'cat and mouse' game continued for several blocks before the black car pulled into the parking garage of a high-rise office building.

One of Sandy's plain-clothes police officers got out and walked into the building in time to observe the elevator doors close behind the crooks and rise to the

8th floor. He informed Sandy and the other officer and, together they boarded another elevator to the 8th floor. They arrived just in time to see the three men enter a room at the end of the hall.

"OK, Bart, we'll camp out here while you call it in. Lawyer Endicott has the search and arrest paperwork all ready,. All he needs is the address and the judge's signature and we can swoop in on these bums and haul them off!" Sandy whispered.

It took only a few minutes for the warrants and Lawyer Endicott gave the word for them to move in!

The prisoners were dumbfounded as to how they had slipped up, and the cop told them:

"When Detective Sandy Sanchez de Torrez got on the case your goose was cooked!"

TWO

Sandy locked up the office and returned to her beachside apartment, but with still a couple hours of daylight left, she decided to do a little surfing. The 'tropical depression' had departed the area but had stirred up some gorgeous waves for 'boarding'.

She was an expert rider of the waves, having been raised near the Costa Rica sandy coast where she learned the art of staying upright on a board charging swiftly over the crest of the huge waves of the Pacific.

A quick change into her tiny flowered bikini, and slipping into a beach robe, she strolled down to the beach and prepared to battle the huge waves rolling in from the Atlantic.

Her olive-toned skin and flowing dark-auburn hair attracted the stares of those already on the beach. But she was oblivious to the hungry eyes of the male bathers, and threw her board into the surf and paddled out to catch her first wave.

She was 'in her element'!

After catching a half-dozen 9 10 foot waves she gathered up her swim gear and returned to her apartment for a shower and a quickly prepared dinner.

As she dried off from her bath, she couldn't help but glance into the full-length mirror to assess the shapely body that had attracted such attention on the beach.

*"**Huh!** Not bad for a thirty-five year old broad even if I do say so, myself!"* she muttered.

The morning presented her with another case on her priority list. This one was a missing person search which, because the person was an adult, the local police had put low importance on the case and had exhausted their limited efforts to find him.

What made a difference to Sandy was, the man was suffering from dementia and had most likely just wandered off from his Senior Assisted Living apartment and couldn't find his way back.

This case struck home with her because her Grandfather also was cursed with the same disease and was frequently getting disoriented. Because he lived in a small village in Costa Rica, most of the people knew him and would gently escort him back home when he got 'lost'.

Sandy's first move was to spend a day with the missing man's relations to determine how serious his problem is and to find out his history of wandering off.

"Are there any neighbors or places he often visited in the past before his dementia became serious?" was Sandy's first question. "Old habits often influence a patient's limited thinking. I'm sure you've already checked those places, but he could still wander back to one of those locations. I'll want a list of all his former familiar 'haunts'".

With this as a starting point, Sandy and two former Miami policemen whom Sandy often temporarily hired to assist her, set off to canvass all the locations on the list. They made extensive searches of the spots where he could have taken shelter. Yard sheds, under porches, dumpsters any place a human or animal could crawl into for shelter.

They expanded their search efforts in a wider and wider area where he was last seen. One of the men even removed a street drainage grate and shone his flashlight down into it's depths. No sign of David down there!

Sandy was on the verge of expanding the search another five blocks in all directions when she received a call on her cel phone.

It was from the director of the Senior Living Facility.

"Detective Sanchez, we just got a call from the manager of a restaurant on the beach. I'm going to forward the call to you so you get the correct info first-hand.

"Hello, this is Detective Sanchez of **P.I. inc.** You have some information for us?"

"I think so. One of my bus-boys was putting some trash in the dumpster this morning and discovered a man digging for scraps of food. He took pity on him and brought him in the kitchen and set him a plate and some beverage. We've been trying to ask him questions but he doesn't seem to know who he is or where he belongs.

"We found a scrap of paper in his pocket with this telephone number scrawled on it. We weren't sure if it was a relatives number, a 'dial-a-date', or a 'morning prayer' number, or what so we called it and got the Senior Living Home," The restaurant manager reported.

"Sir, He just may be a man who has been missing for ten days. Can he tell you his name?"

"No, He doesn't seem to have any awareness of who he is."

"Can you describe him?..."

"Well, he's about 6 feet tall, slim, blue eyes, silver-grey hair with a bald spot on the top

"Ask him if his name might be 'David'," Sandy suggested.

"He says that might be his first or last name..."

"I think he might be the missing man we're looking for. The name thing makes me think so. His name would be 'David Davis' Keep him there and we'll be right over to check him out!"

"Will do! He's a pleasant old gent and is not making any trouble. I sure hope he's your missing man!"

Sandy sped over to the restaurant and, on entering, was relieved to see their missing Senior citizen calmly munching on a slice of toast and washing it down with orange juice.

"Well, Young man, you gave everyone a big scare. I'm sure glad to see you're OK. Now let's get you back home.

"Sir," she addressed the manger, "Please thank your bus-boy for his thoughtfulness. There was a reward posted for Mr. Davis's return and I'll see that the boy gets it"

Sandy placed Mr. Davis in her car and drove him back to the waiting staff and resident friends at the Home.

Sandy's farewell was accompanied by her admonition to Mr. Davis:

"In the future, David, have someone go with you when you decide to go for a stroll, OK?"

Back at the office of **P.I. inc.,** Sandy was happy to write 'closed' to this case.

Next on the priority list

This one involved a client who had a copyright infringement complaint.

Sandy picked up the phone and called the number listed in the e-mail.

"Hi, this is Sandy Sanchez of **P.I., inc.** answering you query about investigating a copyright infringement charge."

"Great! My name's Bart Cole and I need help in settling this mess. I'm a part-time lyricist trying to market my song lyrics and I've learned that a couple of works have been 'pirated' by some obscure recording company. I need proof that I'm the legal owner of these words.

"I had them copyrighted two or three years ago and have been 'hawking' them around to various singers and song publishers. I've had a few favorable comments about some of them but they still remain unpublished.

"Now this two-bit company is marketing a couple as though they owned the rights."

"I'm not an expert in copyright law, but I have a lawyer friend who can assist me," Sandy replied. "I'm sure, between the two us we can nip this in the butt I mean 'BUD'!"

"**I sure <u>hope so.</u>** I've been trying to break into the song-writing business for over a decade and this could ruin me," Bart stated

"Give us a few days and we should have your problem resolved and this shady publisher out of business for good!," Sandy assured him, "I'll need copies of the lyric sheets involved"

"I'll messenger then over to your office this afternoon,"

The next morning Sandy arrived at Attorney Endicott's office with materials in hand.

"Counselor, I've studied these over and they're pretty good. Do you think we can do anything for him?"

"If he has valid copyrights to them it shouldn't be any problem." the lawyer answered.

"This is the CD with the lyrics and the Certificates of Copyright are in the packages I brought over, Sir," Sandy replied.

"Good. Give me the rest of the day to study these things and we'll proceed from there."

Sandy left and lawyer Endicott sat down to peruse the lyrics and the Copyright Certificates..

Loading up the CD he he studied the first set of lyrics

It was a light-hearted country song titled "Lost in Old Mexico"

"I packed up my '48 Woodie and headed west for
San Francisco
I had a 'gig' to play in that city on the Bay
my first really 'big sho'
But somewhere east of Amarillo I
took a wrong fork in the road.
OH, I really blew it, 'cause before I knew it
I was deep in Old Mexico!

chorus-
>   I'm a Tennessee gringo, who can't speak
>   The lingo,
>   Lost in Old Mexico."   (¹)

There followed several similar verses. When the lawyer finished he sat back and mused:

"*I'm no music critic, but it sounds good to me. This guy <u>could</u> make it, if the right musician put it to music and the right artist recorded it.*" was his reaction.

He picket up the phone and called Sandy.

"Hi, Beautiful, I just finished examining the info you left off and I think you should go ahead with your investigation of the recording company involved. Mr. Cole has a legitimate case of infringement as far as I can see. Sock it 'em, Gal."

Sandy's first move was a computer search for the recording company that had recorded made the pirated song. The BBB had no listing for them and the ICC (International Composers' Coalition) only reported them as an obscure company with limited assets and no records on the 'hit list'. From the search Sandy was able to get an address which listed the company at 2254 International Drive, Tijuana, Mexico S.A.

When Sandy reported her findings to Attorney Endicott, he informed her:

"Sandy, Gal, I'm afraid, with the crooks operating in Mexico, there isn't much we can do except get an injunction against them peddling the record in the US. Collecting any money would require filing a claim in

---

¹)   Lyrics by the author © 2005

the Mexican courts, which would probably cost more than Bart Cole would be able to collect. I'm sorry."

"Well, Counselor, we tried," Sandy couldn't hide her disappointment.

"Can we help him get his work published in the US?"

"I'll contact some of my fellow attorneys who handle artists and entertainers. Maybe one of them can put him with someone who can help him."

"Thank you, Man, I'd sure like to see him live his dream!"

Sandy marked this one off as a '**Losewin'** case

THREE

Returning to her apartment, Sandy adjourned to the beach to again enjoy surfing and sunbathing. Her olive-toned skin required no tanning to give her that 'beach-bunny' complexion for which the rest of the sun-worshippers on the beach were striving so hard to achieve..

After an hour of strenuous boarding, Sandy lounged on her blanket to 'recharge her batteries', while the gentle coastal breezes evaporated the sparkling droplets of ocean water collected on her silky-soft body.

She was fiully aware of the hot glances sent her way by the men on the beach, as they nonchalantly strolled by. It seemed every male on the beach found an excuse to pass by her reclining figure to enjoy the view.

Her rock-hard breasts fairly bursting out of their flimsy restraint and the tiny bikini thong adhering to her mons pubis stirred the blood of every male observing her beauty.

Sandy was also actually getting aroused by the hot stares. She hadn't had a man for some time and her imagination was stirring thoughts of what coupling had been like.

"I gotta' stop thinking these erotic thoughts or else find a MAN," she mentally admonished herself.

She gathered up her blanket and surf board and headed for a <u>Cold shower</u>, while her shaky legs could still carry her..

Back to work the next morning, Sandy booted up her computer to check for her next assignment.

She dialed the phone number listed in her next e-mail on her priority list A male voice answered:

"Good morning, this is the office of Attorney Alvin Klein, how can I help you?"

"Well, Sir, I'm calling in response to your e-mail requesting **My** help. This is Detective Sanchez of **P.I., inc.**" Sandy responded, "I assume you have a case for us?"

"Oh, good! Thanks for returning my query, M'am. Here's the situation I'm the executor of a very ample estate and I need to locate the beneficiary of a large part of the assets.. Can you help me?"

"First, Counselor, I'm about forty years short of being a 'M'am'. My name is Sandy and I'm sure we can work with you on this." Sandy replied with a smile in her voice.

"My apologies, Sandy. My offices are in Hialeah Gardens. Would you like to meet here or at your place, to go over the details?"

"I think it'd be more convenient to meet at my office," Sandy answered, "That way I can 'download' all the info to my files as you lay it out."

"OK, I'll see you this afternoon if that's all right with you?"

"Great, I'll see you then."

Attorney Klein arrived, briefcase in hand, and Sandy showed him to a seat in the small conference room.

"First off, Sandy, I'll give you some background

"My client was a Marine in the Korean 'Conflict' and was at the Chosen Reservoir where he had both of his feet frost-bit'. His Squad Leader carried him on his back for three days during their evacuation march from the Reservoir to Hungnam. When they arrived at the harbor, the Corporal deposited his cargo on a Navy Hospital Ship and then rejoined his squad on an LST for transport to Pusan.

"My client never saw his buddy again and lost track of him, until, three years ago when he received a Christmas card from him. He had retired and was then living in a Veterans' home somewhere on the Gulf Coast.

"In the meantime, my client had gone into business in 'Little Havana' and opened up a chain of mini-marts which grew and made him a millionaire.

"When he died he bequeathed three million dollars (that's with an 'M'!) to various veterans' associations and the remaining **two million** he left to his savior in Korea!

"What I need you to do is locate Staff Sergeant Clyde Odem so I can unload this check on him!" Attorney Klein calmly announced.

"**WHEW!**" Sandy huffed, "That's some chunk of cash! I'll drop everything and get right on it. I just hope he's still alive and can enjoy it!"

"So do I!"

Sandy's immediate move was to get on the VA data base and see what they might have on the Sergeant.. This was only mildly successful. The VA records only carried him up to two years ago then he dropped off their radar.

A search of Veterans' homes on the Gulf Coast also produced negative results. One home did have a listing that showed he had a son living in Jackson Mississippi.

Sandy 'Googled' up the son's name in the Jackson telephone listings but found no active account there either.

"By golly, you can hide, but Sandy"ll dig till she finds you!" Sandy muttered to herself.

Just when Sandy's determination was growing thin she received a call.!

"I heard you're looking for my Dad," the male voice on the other end asked.

"If his name is Staff Sergeant Clyde Odem, US Marine Corps Retired, then I **SURE AM!**" Sandy shouted.

"Well, he's living with me here in Coral Springs. He's now eighty years old but still spry as I am! What's he wanted for?"

"Hold on to your bonnet, Junior, he's heir to a bundle of cash. Get pencil and paper and I'll give you the Lawyer's address and phone number and he'll tell you all about it after he verify's your dad's ID.!

"HOLY JUMPIN' HORN TOADS!" the voice on the phone nearly deafened Sandy.

As soon as she hung up, Sandy called Attorney Klein to give him the news.

"I sure hope he's our man, Counselor. It sounds to me like we've found him!"

"I certainly hope so!"

"You know, Detective, **inheriting** $2 Million is better than hitting the Lottery for $2 Million with the lottery Uncle Sam takes a BIG bite in taxes but inheriting $2 Million is TAX FREE up to $5,340,000!" the

Attorney informed Sandy,. "Therefore the Sergeant gets the whole shebang!"

"Good on him!" Sandy remarked

The veteran Staff Sergeant was able to provide his DD 214 Record of Service to prove he was the hero from the Chosen Reservoir March. So attorney Klein was able to present him with a certified check for $2 M..

With an intense feeling of satisfaction, Sandy closed up the offices of **P.I., inc.** and retired to the nearby 'Bistro' for dinner and a Magnum of Champagne to celebrate a job 'Well Done' <u>on Attorney Klein!</u> of course!

FOUR

Sandy's list was growing shorter with each case being solved.

Perusing the requests, Sandy found most of the items involved simple background checks and marital disputes.

"These should be easy to dispose of without too much 'leg-work'," She mused, and adjourned to her computer.

Lawyer Endicott had another assignment for her a divorcee who was trying to locater her 'ex' who was eight months in arrears on his child support payments.

Sandy contacted the lawyer for details.

"Hi, Counselor, what's the 'skinny' on this dead-beat so I can track him down for you?" she began.

"Well, as I said in my e-mail, he has a court-ordered child support judgment against him and has defaulted on his payments for the last eight months. His spouse has tried to locate him but he's in hiding. She needs help in locating him."

"Counselor, if there's anything that pisses me off worse, it's someone who doesn't meet his obligations to his children!" Sandy hissed, "I'll take this case pro bono, just to have the pleasure of kicking this guy's butt when I find him!"

"No need to take it 'on the cuff'," Gal." The lawyer replied, "We'll stick him with your bill as well as collect his back-dues, when we catch him!"

"That's all well and good, but I'd still like to put my boot to his rear!" Sandy laughed.

"Me, too!"

Sandy began her usual search of the internet. Phone directories, utility companies, bank accounts, credit companies and any other data bases that might reveal the location of the debtor.

Sandy brought into play some of Andy's original computer programs. one of which listed drivers' licenses, car registrations and credit card listings.

EUREKA! Master Card files had a listing for the name and address of the miscreant!

"We GOTCHA', You Cheap Bastard, you," Sandy exclaimed as the information came up on her computer screen.

She quickly informed Lawyer Endicott of her success.

"I'm going to head over to the address and see if it's really him and if he still lives there. I'll let yoi know what I find and you can take over the action from there."

"Suits me fine, Detective. God luck!"

On the hour-long drive to the deadbeat's home Sandy was all aquiver in anticipation. She made a brief circle around the residence and proceeded to knock on a few doors in the vicinity and questioned some of the neighbors. She showed his picture around in order to ascertain if he was, indeed, her target.

With the identification confirmed, Sandy contacted Lawyer Endicott with the news.

"Counselor, WE GOT HIM. Now start your legal mumbo-jumbo and stick it to him! I can't wait to see that ex wife and children make him pay up!" said Sandy, hardly able to restrain her exuberance.

"It's times like these that make me proud of being a 'Snoop'!"
Sandy thought to herself."

A missing person became her next project. The husband of a prominent Miami socialite had came to the office seeking **P.I., inc.**'s help in finding his wife.

"This will have to be handled very discreetly. I'm Erick Storm. I am CEO of 'Storm Enterprises' and this could effect the integrity of my firm if it's handled wrong. That's why I'm asking for your help and not going to the police.

"She had been corresponding with someone on the internet male or female I have no idea and I believe she may have gone somewhere to meet this party," the man told Sandy.

"Sir," Sandy replied, "The first thing I'll want is access to her computer. With my computer programs I'll be able to find out who the person is with whom she was corresponding. Knowing that we can 'back-track' and start our investigating of the other person," Sandy advised him.

"Anything you need, Detective. All my company and personal recourses are at your disposal!" Mr. Storm volunteered.

When Sandy started digging through the wife's computer history she eventually narrowed the e-mail trail down to a woman in Charleston, SC.

"I can't guarantee she has anything to do with your wife's disappearance, but she could <u>know </u>where she went," Sandy reassured the client.

"I have a friend in the Charleston police department who I can trust to keep this confidential and he'll do a little checking on that end. I'll let you know what he finds out."

"That sounds great to me. I'm at my wit's end with worry. I keep praying Eleanor is alive and well." Erick said.

"We'll all be praying the same thing, Sir."

Sandy put in a phone call to her Charleston contact. As briefly as she could she explained the problem.

"I'll get right on it, Sandy. I should have news for you before day's end. I'll call you back this evening."

Sandy was waiting anxiously for that call and, when her cel-phone rang, she quickly answered:

"Hello, **P.I., inc.**"

"Hi, gal, I have good news and bad news for you! Your missing woman is here in Charleston, alive and well. The bad news is, she says she intends to stay here! She says she's grown tired of the as she put it 'Snooty Miami crowd' she was surrounded by. All that high society living just wasn't her 'cup-o-tea'!

"She grew up in a small town in Carolina and all that money and luxuries didn't impress her one bit!"

Sandy had the sad task of reporting her findings to the client.

"I'm so sorry, Erick, but at least she's safe!"

FIVE

Sandy assumed, since this case was a 'wrap' and she could relax for a day or two but to 'assume' anything only makes an 'Ass out of you and Me! She was sadly mistaken!

Opening her morning mail, she found a crudely composed letter which shook her world!

Letters cut from the local newspaper and glued to an.8 ½ X 11 sheet of stationary spelled out a disturbing threat:

'Bitch You've meddled into something you shouldn't have and you'll pay for it,! You'd best carry a gun cause you're going to need it. I'm going to kill you!!'

The postmark indicated it was mailed from the city where Sandy had tracked the 'deadbeat'. child support father, and with her AFIS (finger print identifier) program, she was able to compare prints on the stationary to those of the 'deadbeat'.

Sandy called Patrick, her former co-detective and founder of **P.I., inc.**

"Pat, what do you suggest I do.? I'm not afraid of this bastard but I don't relish an ambush or a 'wild west shootout' either!" she told him.

"Something like this, it's best to make the first move." Patrick advised, "He's going to figure he's got you scared, so if you go after him it's going to throw him off-guard.

"Pick up a couple of your Miami Swat Team buddies and set up a 'sting'! He won't be expecting you to take the initiative and the three of you should be able to take him down without a shoot out!" Patrick suggested

"I sure hope it works, Partner!"

Locating the gunman was simple since he was not expecting his victim to be the first to attack. As with most crooks he hadn't counted on her to react as she did.

Sandy and the two Swat-Team officers arrive at the home of the culprit, with warrants in hand, just after sundown and took him completely off guard. He was taken away in handcuffs and charged with making a felonious threat. In addition, since the threat was sent through the US Mails, he faces federal charges, too!

Sandy was able to breath a sigh of relief after this case was resolved and the danger was removed.

The remaining couple of cases were simple background investigations of prospective employees which companies needed before hiring the new personnel. Sandy wrapped them up in a single day and decided to take the rest of the week off.

Her main relaxation was more time surfing and lounging in the Miami sun.

"I'm going to <u>have</u> to get me a <u>one-piece </u>bathing suit if I'm going to spend much time on the beach." Sandy chided herself. *"I attract too many lascivious ogles in my bikini. All*

this attention stirs too many erotic desires in the onlookers as well in ME!".

Sandy couldn't help but notice one particular fellow-surfer lying on a nearby beach towel. He was a slightly-tanned vision of male physical perfection. With abs that resembled an old fashioned wash-board, and well defined muscles in his arms and legs, the result of years of surfing and exercise, Sandy found it hard to take her eyes off him.

"WOW!" Sandy thought to herself, *"That's a guy I could go for!"*

Her attention did not go unnoticed by the 'Adonis' nearby.

After a half-hour of exchanging glances, the man got up from his beach-towel and sauntered over to Sandy's location and spoke:

"I've watched you surf and see you really know how to handle a 'board'.

You must have been at it for a while. My name's José Ramos. I hope I'm not offending you, but seeing you here several times, I just had to meet you."

"No offense, José," Sandy replied, "I'm Sandy, I've noticed you on your board, too., and it's exciting to watch you work the waves. I'm glad to finally meet you."

"Not to be too forward, but would you like to go for a drink and dinner with me this *evening?"*

"Well, not to seem too 'easy', I'd love to!" Sandy laughed.

"Ah! A sense of humor I love that in a woman!"

"I'll retire to my apartment and change into street clothes, and meet you in twenty minutes."

"Great! That restaurant on the corner over there is very good. I'll see you there in twenty," José kissed her hand as they parted, temporarily.

Sandy was so flustered she had difficulty exchanging her bikini for dress slacks and halter.

"What am I doing?" she muttered, *"I just met the guy and already I'm contemplating how he'd be IN BED!"*

The dinner was excellent but Sandy hardly tasted it her appetite was elsewhere.

Arriving at her apartment door Sandy and José locked lips and it was with reluctance she bid him: "See you tomorrow, Good Night," and left him standing in the hall.

"GADS,!" She said, *"I wanted to bed him, but I'm not loose and **my rule is: never on the first date**! DAMMIT!"*

SIX

Sandy found very little time to reflect on the events of last night

She unlocked the door and was taking her first sip of Cuban coffee when the strident ringing of the phone grabbed her attention.

"Sandy, I got a hot one for you!" Attorney Endicott exclaimed, "I have a client who urgently needs your services!

"A young lady client, a local psychiatrist, is the target of a 'stalker' and is seeking a body-guard 24/7. She knows the stalker. He's a former patient she had been treating for extreme psychosis and had "Baker Acted' him twice, but he had checked himself out of the clinic as soon as the mandatory 72 hours had expired.

After she found him stalking and harassing her, she went to the police but the police won't move on him until he actually acts against her. By that time she fears it'll be too late! His brother says he owns several fire-arms and he has no doubt he wouldn't hesitate to use them!".

"**Jeez!**" Sandy muttered, "I can't imagine the police just standing by while her life is obviously in danger!"

"That's one of the injustices of the law," Endicott replied, "Their hands are tied. Until he makes an illegal move they have to keep 'hands off!"

"Well, Counselor you can count me in. Give me the details and I'll put this on the top of my list.!"

"I knew I could rely on you. I'll let her know you're coming. I can fax you her number and address and all the info and you can take it from there."

"Will do!"

Sandy followed up on the address and proceeded to the young lady's home to take up watch against the stalker.

She came prepared with he own weapons, a 9 mm Berretta and a protective vest. Sandy was a former Marine MP and was a crack shot and not averse to using bullets to quell any aggressive attack by the culprit.

"I'm Detective Sandy Sanchez," she introduced herself to the client,   "I'm going to be your shadow 24/7. For your safety, I have a few rules which you must abide by.

"Number one stay away from the windows, keep the blinds closed, never open the door (I'll handle that!)

"Number two you never leave the house until I first. check the street. I'm placing video surveillance cameras around the house perimeter so we'll see if any intruder approaches.

"If, when we're outside, you hear me say **DROP!** I want you flat on your stomach with your hands covering your head.

"You follow these rules and you have the best chance of surviving any attack on your life," Sandy advised her.

"**LORDY!** Detective, you make it sound like a **war!**"

"Missy, **IT IS!** Sandy emphasized., "and it'll go on until this guy is put down or behind bars!"

For the next two days, no harassing phone calls and no alarms from the surveillance cameras except for one early morning alert of an intruder on the southeast corner of the house which, when Sandy made a cautious inspection, proved to be only a neighbor taking his German Shepherd for his morning stroll.

Another 24 hours and still no action.

Then the phone ringing brought Sandy to full alert! She picked up the receiver and answered:

"Hello, can I help you?"

The voice on the other end spoke in what was obviously a distorted tone:

"You think you can hide from me? Don't kid yourself! I know where you live and I'll be paying you a visit very shortly!"

"Don't kid yourself, Buster, I'm ready for you. Your fun days are over!" Sandy returned his threat.

She hung up and turned to her client

"I think he thought he was talking to you, which is good! Now we go into 'action mode' and be ready to surprise him when he makes his move."

Sandy's next move was to called the local police and informed them of the development.

"There'll probably be some gun play and I want your people to be close by to move in swiftly," she informed the desk sergeant, "I don't plan to fire first, but at the first shot from this mug, I intend to put him down and I need witnesses that I fired in self defense."

"We'll send a SWAT team over and have the house in our sights at all times," the Sergeant assured her, "Good luck!"

The street was quiet until just after sundown when surveillance cameras on the back side of the house sounded the alarm 'intruder on the move'!

Sandy instructed her client to lie down between the rear wall and the sofa.

"And don't come out until I give the 'All Clear'!"

Sandy checked her Barretta and slipped towards the back door. As she cautiously moved through the darkened kitchen she saw a shadow at the door. She waited while he jimmied the lock and was slipping into the kitchen - then she spoke in her loudest and most commanding voice:

<u>STOP WHERE YOU ARE AND DROP YOUR WEAPON!</u>

The intruder made a dive for the door but Sandy kicked it closed in his face. His only escape blocked, he turned and fired off three shots into the darkened room. Not knowing where his target was, his bullets went ricocheting wildly around the room. Sandy had taken shelter behind the refrigerator and chips flying from the appliance added to the shrapnel winging about the kitchen.

Sandy fired one shot at the silhouetted figure and he dropped to the kitchen floor with a 'thud'

She quickly hit the light switch and kicked the crooks weapon out of his reach.

The echo of the gunfire was still reverberating in the kitchen when the five-man SWAT team came bursting through the closed door.

"Sergeant, I gave him a chance to lay down his pistol but he chose the hard way out. Check him over but I think you'll find I put my shot right in his gullet,"

Sandy said., "I had only his silhouette to shoot at but, it was just like those targets in the range!"

"OH, GAL! You scored a bulls eye this time! He was dead before he hit the floor!

With the elimination of the 'stalker', Sandy's 24/7 guard duty ended and she returned to her apartment for a shower and a change of clothes.

As much as she wanted, it was too late for a dip in the ocean, so she rustled up a snack and crawled into her Beauty Rest to 'recharge her batteries'.

Her 24-hour, four-day vigil left Sandy with no time to think of other things, plus the couple of days of police questioning and 'shooting involved'

Investigation, consumed all her thoughts. The Board of Review determined that the killing was justified and classified it as 'self-defense', so Sandy was exonerated of responsibility.

A sound night's sleep and Sandy returned to the office to find her computer crammed with e-mails and her answering machine full of messages, several from José. He was unaware of her occupation and therefore had no idea why she was 'incommunicado'.

Sandy decided she needed to know more about him if they were going to pursue a 'relationship', so she went to her computer and did a brief search.

His record was 'squeaky clean' not even a traffic ticket! As for his occupation, José was quite wealthy. He had a Photography studio on South.

Beach. where he made a very good living shooting glamour, 'boudoir' and high fashion pics for many of Miami's rich ladies who came to him for sexy photos of themselves to present to their husbands (or 'gigolo' paramours).

They paid very high premiums for his discretion and for his excellent work..

He was also on the 'contributor' list of several prestigious women's magazines that used much of his fashion shots.

"WELL!" Sandy muttered, "*All those sex-starved broads around, and you set your sights on me? I'll have to make you sweat, if you want to 'get in my pants!'*"

The news didn't curb Sandy's own desire but only made her more determined that this was **not** going to be a 'one-night-stand'!

Sandy sorted through her batch of e-mails and printed up the two or three that held promise of being investigative material and deleted the remainder.

The phone messages received the same treatment and she wound up with only two seeking her services. There were five from José which she put at the top of her list.

Sandy made a note to call him after she took care of checking the new cases on her computer and answering machine. All but one of her e-mails involved only on-line dating background checks. bottom of the list! These could wait.

The two answering machine messages were both from lawyer clients.

One, looking for a missing person, the other was a marital dispute case. Sandy classed neither as high priority.

Having set all these cases aside Sandy picked up her phone and called José.

"Hi ya, 'Beach Bum', got your messages but was away on a job so am just now catching up," Sandy greeted him.

"What the blazes kind of a 'job' do you have that takes you away for almost two weeks ? You some kinda' airline stew or something?" he inquired.

"No. Nothing like that" Sandy laughed, "Let's do dinner tonight and I'll tell you all about it."

"That sounds great. Where'd you like to go?"

"How does Brazilian Bar-B-Que sound to you? My ex-boss took me to a great place along the Inland Waterway that serves what's called Churrascaria (sp.). "It's **big** chunks of beef cooked over a huge open pit. The waiter passes among the tables with a big slab of meat and slices off whopping pieces on your plate. It's de-e-e-licious!"

"You're on, Gal! Just hearing you describe it has me salivating already!

I'll pick you up at seven with my knife and fork in hand!"

When José arrived to pick up Sandy, she was taken aback when she saw the car he was driving

"Holy Cow!" she exclaimed, "A Classic '57 Chevy Bel Air!"

"Yeah. When my business started 'booming' that was one of the first personal luxuries I bought. It's completely restored, inside and out, with a couple of added changes power steering, power brakes, reworked suspension, and a 'Bose'™ stereo system and 'Blue-Ray'™ CD player..

Crank. that up and you'd swear you're in the 5th row in Carnegie Hall!"

"Just what kind of work do you do, anyway?" Sandy asked, "I did a miner classified background check on you that only said you were a photographer.".

"Yeah, I own a photo studio on South Beach. I've built it into quite a profitable business. I specialize in fashion, glamour and 'boudoir' photography and cater to some of the 'rich-bitches' of Miami." he replied.

"They fork over a nice bundle to have 'sexy' pictures made of them. to present to their husbands (and their 'gigolo' paramours)," he chuckled.

"Sounds like fun," Sandy replied.

"Interesting, but not always 'fun'!" José corrected, "some of them can get pretty critical. and demanding!" José said. "While we're baring our souls, what is it you do that puts you unreachable for a week or more?"

"I'm a private investigator. I have my own agency **P.I., inc.**" Sandy answered, "I'm a 'snoop', you might say!"

"And you say my work 'sound like fun'!"

"I'd really like to see your studio, sometime,"

"Tomorrow I have no scheduled appointments, so why don't I give you the 'cook's' tour?"

"That' a date, Señor!' Sandy quipped. .

The meal was everything Sandy had described and, with an excellent bottle of red wine and a fresh palm-hearts salad, it put the evening on track for being a resounding success.

The restaurant had an outdoor veranda where they dined in view of the Atlantic Ocean with the soft, gentle breezes caressing them as they enjoyed the repast.

Following the meal, they remained on the veranda sipping their after- dinner brandies and watching the moonlight sparkling on the breaking surf.

This all added up to a VERY ROMANTIC end to the evening.

José drove Sandy back to her apartment and, again she bid him "Good Night" after a soul-searing kiss.

"I would invite you in, but let's see where we're going before we get too serious, OK?"

"If you say so, Darlin', but my ego is getting 'bruised' with your 'kiss and run' treatment. Wherever this relationship is headed I'm sure the reward, in the end, is going to be worth the wait!"

"Oh, I'm sure it WILL BE!" Sandy chuckled.

SEVEN

Sandy had barely finished her first cup of coffee and sat down to her computer, when her phone jarred her back to the reality of the day

"Hello, this is **P.I. inc.,** How may I be of service to you?"

"Now ain't you the business-like Lady?" José laughed into the receiver.

"And the 'top- o-the -morning' to you, too. What are you up to this early in the day?"

"I promised you a tour of the studios of '**Glamour by José**' so, if you can spare a coupler hours, I'll pick you up and I'll show you my 'hole in the Wall'. Whatta' you say?"

"Give me two hours to clear up a few details here and I'll be happy to go with you."

"See you about ten-ish then, Darlin;!"

Sandy was able to clear a couple of background check requests from her calendar and was ready to visit Josè's studio.

The place he had referred to as his 'hole-in-the-wall' was anything BUT!

His studio occupied the entire ground floor of the beach-front building!.

The inside layout included two 30' X 40' camera rooms one for routine photos and the other containing an entire wall of 'green-screen' for composite photos, (where various scenes can be electronically projected into the photo background behind the subject as is done on TV for the weatherman's maps).

Three dressing and makeup rooms, one large storage room for sets and props, a computer room where the photos are 'doctored', downloaded and printed, take up the remainder of the ground-floor space, with only a small 10' X 10' corner set aside for office work.

"I have four top-notch assistants who are the backbone of this operation," He told Sandy, "One woman, Audry, my stylist who handles wardrobe, make-up and hair, and another woman Marge, who's the best in the business at 'Photoshopping' the images to remove wrinkles, blemishes, stray hairs and, often, removing a <u>few extra pounds</u>! She can make the ugliest of women look like Marilyn Monroe" José chuckled.

"The other two are 'muscle-men' who jockey the large sets and props around and assist me in setting the lights."

"WOW!!" Sandy marveled at the enormity of the place. "You're **too** modest 'hole-in-the-wall' my Aunt Matilda's girdle! This place is stupend- ous!".

"It cost a pretty penny but I own it outright along with the penthouse on the roof. all paid for courtesy of Miami's **<u>female vanity!</u>**"

Needless to say, Sandy was **<u>impressed!!</u>**

"I'd like to work some of my camera magic on you one of these days,

'Gorgeous'," José approached Sandy.

"It's a tantalizing offer, but I'm a private investigator and that doesn't suit the image I want to project, thank you."

"You're more beautiful than any of the females I've photographed, so far" José declared, "You'd be a 'knockout' even before Marge did any 'Photo- shopping' to the images I could produce!"

"Very flattering, but still, thanks, but, no thanks."

"Suit yourself. But if you ever change your mind, the offer stands."

"Since you're giving me the 'grand tour', how about letting me see the penthouse?" Sandy asked.

The building housed two elevators. One express elevator direct to the penthouse which required a 'password' to activate, and the other serviced the other five floors which contained two apartments per floor. These were owned or rented by various prominent Miami businessmen Sandy was whisked to José's rooftop penthouse where she received another shock! In addition to elaborate living facilities, there was a 15' X 60' swimming pool!

"I sometimes use the pool for my swim-suit shots so I'm able to write it off as a 'business expense'," José laughed.

"Them that has money, makes money!" Sandy chided him.

"Yeah,. In my case, You can say that. I live a good life which leaves nothing lacking.

"Enough braggin' about me! if you don't have anything demanding your time and attention, what say to lunch and an afternoon at the beach riding the boards.? The weatherman says the surf is UP!"

"I'd love that!" Sandy agreed.

The rest of the day was filled with surf-boarding and basking in the Florida Sun.

Dinner at one of South Beach's sidewalk restaurants completed the day and José drove Sandy back to her apartment.

This time Sandy invited him in 'for coffee' and they spent a very romantic few hours before Sandy advised José:

"It's still too soon for me to invite you to spend the night but don't get discouraged. I'm just cautious but as anxious as you are!"

"I truly doubt that, 'Sweetheart', But I'll wait **forever!** if that's what it Takes!"

José went back to his penthouse with an ache in his groin, and was doomed throughout the night to enduring his desire only in his dreams!

It was 'Spring Break' and the beaches swarmed with young vacationers, and restaurants and motels were packed.

"This is a good time to concentrate on my case-load and hole-up in my office and apartment," Sandy decided, *"Leave Miami's beaches and attractions to the wild college crowd!"*

On Sandy's return to the office, she found a new message on her e-mail.

"I was recommended to your agency by Attorney. Endicott. I'm a 'scout' for a minor league ball team and have my eye on a prime pitching candidate, but need to know more about him before I commit," the message read.

"Lawyer Endicott says you can find out all the skeletons in his closet, from how he ties his shoes to what size jock-strap he wears !"

"Call me so we can discuss this matter."

The e-mail ended with the scout's phone number so Sandy picked up the phone and dialed it.

"This is detective Sandy Sanchez of **P.I., inc.,**" Sandy announced herself, "I got your e-mail and I think I can probably help dig up any dirt in your pitcher's personal life **except the 'jock-strap size',**. "That's a little **too personal**!" Sandy chuckled, "Other than that, when I get through, you'll know more about him than his mother!"

"Then, Misses Sanchez, we have a deal. Tell me what you need and I'll fax you all we have here!"

"That'll be fine, and call me 'Sandy', my kind of work calls for a more informal relationship."

"OK, then you can call me 'Brett' (my full handle is 'Brett Sanders')", he returned.

When the faxed information arrived, Sandy immediately went to work on her computer searching for anything that might be on the internet. She found nothing there, other that the report Brett had sent her.

That being a dead-end, she started looking for close friends and relatives who might shed any light on the pitcher. She made a list of their names and addresses and set off to start interrogating (interviewing) them.

Those living in the south Florida area were placed at the top of her list.

The subject of her search had no siblings in Florida so she began her questioning with close friends.

As she proceeded from one to another, she was getting a picture of a 'squeaky-clean' young college athlete who had few ties with female students.

He was majoring in Public Relations and had an above average IQ. no 'dirt' there! He was not ardently religious but appeared to pretty much live by the 'Golden Rule'. He was spoken well of by faculty and fellow students.

Sandy was beginning to think she was investigating a **'Saint'**.

No drug history.!

No gambling

No police record!

No school discipline problems!

"Damn! This guy is almost too good to be true." Sandy mused, *"I'm beginning to feel Brett's wasting his money hiring my services!"*

Delving further, Sandy found, when asking friends and relations about his childhood, that he had been raised by a Maiden Aunt when, at the age of four, both his parents were taken by Scarlett Fever. She was a strict disciplinarian and he was not a happy child. Due to this upbringing, he grew up a very quiet and studious child.

In high school, he was a top of his class student. He took an interest in baseball and developed an extremely fast curve ball that caught the attention of sports writers and scouts.

It was at this point that Brett came into his life.

Wherever Sandy's search took her, all information was favorable. So, after exhausting all her sources, she reported her findings to Brett.

"Brett, I think you've found your team an outstanding pitcher." she told him, "I did a very thorough search and I found nothing negative about him. Good Luck in the upcoming season!"

The list of pending cases was whittled down to three on-line dating background investigations so Sandy opted to closing them and take some time off.

The first one looked to be a 'routine' check-up until she read further into the folder that's when she discovered it was **far** from **'routine'**! This one was going to take all of Sandy's resources to unravel!

The case involved a lady who signed on to a dating service that did not bother with background checks and relied on the truthfulness of a member's profile.

This allowed an applicant to present himself, or, herself, as something they were not ie - a 69 year old, balding, overweight 'tub of lard' could pass himself off as a 27 year old marathon runner with abs like railroad ties, resembling George Clooney! You pick your choice and take your chance!

She contacted the requestor and set up a face-to-face-meet to go over the details.

"Detective, My name is Margarita Ramos (Rita) and I need help uncovering what I perceive to be a scam using the internet dating service called 'Dream Dates' of which I've been a member over the past seven months.", she began, after arriving at the office of **P.I, inc.**

"For the past five months I'm been carrying on an on-line relationship with a guy who says his name is Richard Warren. Over these months our conversations have developed into a deep feeling of affection, so much so that we've even discussed marriage.

"I know that sounds premature, but we were making plans for him to come to Florida so we could meet!" Rita told Sandy.

"Not so foolish," Sandy replied, "many good marriages have come out of meetings on-line, so what's so different about your case?"

"Well, Sandy, I'm no 'spring chicken'. I'm 71 years old but I'm not senile nor am I suffering from Alzheimer's. or dementia! I've been around and I know when something 'stinks in Denmark'!" Rita added.

"Monday (**?**)Richard(**?**) asked for a **'loan' of $2700** to pay off his 'car loan'! I smell a **scam** here and I want you to look into this man's records before I get taken for a ride!"

"Rita, I'll dig into this guy's past so deep, we'll know if he was a natural birth or cesarean! This sounds like the old 'con' to me, too.

"Give me a week and I should have some news for you by then," Sandy assured her client. "I'll give you a report as soon as I come up with anything.

"Send me copies of the last four month's e-mails, and any letters he wrote to you. Handle the letters with gloves in case I can bring up any prints, and also the envelopes the letters came in DNA from his licking the seal might come in handy in case he has a 'record'!

"That, along with a thorough computer search, ought to reveal all there is to know about your 'Richard Warren'!" Sandy promised.

"Thanks, Sandy. Good luck! I'll be waiting to hear from you."

Sandy's first move was to crank up 'Genius' Andy's computer programs to try to search down the source and identity of the culprit.

Using the information in his e-mails Sandy first had to break through the server's 'Firewalls' to divulge their subscriber list. Getting the list. she then had to go through a process of eliminating names until she boiled it down to reveal the true name of 'Richard'.

This involved diligent computer manipulations taking 48 to 72 hours, but, in the end, she came up with 'Richard's' name and address and further searching revealed he had a 'rap sheet' of fraud cases extending over the last decade

Finger prints obtained from the letters were inconclusive and the DNA on the envelope flaps did not reveal any info. Only the tracing through the server., were records opened up which resulted in revealing 'Richard's' true identity!

Two weeks of Sandy's investigating convinced her that this was now a case for the FCC and federal authorities to bring 'Richard' to justice.

Sandy called Ms. Ramos and reported her findings.

"I think we have what we need to put this bum away for quite a few years, Rita," she informed her, "thanks to your vigilance"

"No! THANKS to **P.I. inc.!** Sandy," Rita corrected her.

EIGHT

With the wrapping-up of the on-line dating fraud case, Sandy turned to her priority list and set to work doing the last background check. This one did prove to be routine and in three hours she had completed it and sent her report to the client.

"It's time for some 'me time' now," she decided, *"I think I'll give José a call and see what we can cook up."*

"Hey, Beautiful! It's about time I heard from you. I've been dreaming about you, but dreams are a poor substitute for the 'real thing'!" José scolded her..

"I've been busy solving crimes, but I'm ready to 'chill out' for a few days now. Got any good ideas?"

"Oh, I'm full of ideas some good, and some 'naughty'."

"Let's start with the 'good' ones first, then later we can tackle the 'NAUGHTY' ones!" Sandy laughed.

"How does this one sound to you? I have a small single-engine amphibian plane sitting over at the West Miami Air Park just waiting to soar into the 'wild blue'," José suggested,

"Let's gas her up and hop over to Bermuda for a few days of R&R? I have a friend owns a shack on the beach and I have a standing invite to use it whenever I want.?"

"I'll just take you up on that idea!" Sandy quickly responded.

"Great! Just throw a bikini, a couple beach-towels and sandals in a bag and I'll pick you up at 11 AM! The surf there isn't much so we can leave the boards here. besides I don't expect we'll have much time for surfing, anyway!!" he laughed

José was an accomplished pilot and the take-off and landing were super smooth. He taxied the small amphibian up to the dock in front of his friend's beach-front cottage.

"Direct to the doorstep delivery, M' lady," He announced.

"WOW! José, is there **anything** you can't do?" Sandy exclaimed.

"Well, we'll see about that tonight!!" he chuckled with a lifting of an eyebrow.

"Now, whatever could you mean by that, Mister?" she asked coyly.

Dinner that night, was delivered from one of the better Bermuda Restaurants, and, with after-dinner cocktails in hand, they moved to the veranda to watch the colorful sunset. .

As the glow slowly faded from the sky, José took Sandy by the hand and walked her back into the house.

"If you're uncomfortable, the cottage has two bedrooms and we can use them both or not your choice."

"I think **only one** will do nicely," Sandy said, "I think I'm ready to crank our relationship up a notch!"

The night was very satisfying (I'll leave the details to your imagination) and Sandy awakened with the tropic sun streaming through the bamboo shutters.

As she stirred, a hand reached over and cupped her right breast.

"Good morning, Angel," José whispered into her ear, "I hope you had a good night. How about a morning dip into that lovely Bermuda water? This part of the beach is private and secluded so no bathing suits required!"

"Sounds wonderful to me. Last one in is a monkey's uncle" Sandy said with a mischievous smirk, jumping out of the sack and making a dash for the shore..

The race to the surf-line was a tie and their bodies were soon awash with the tropic water and the sun warming them in it's golden rays.

Breakfast at a nearby sidewalk lunch stand consisted of exotic fruits and sweet pastries, with strong black coffee to wash it all down.

The remainder of the day was spent between lounging (nude) on the white sand of their private beach and cavorting in the warm Bermuda waters.

Five days and nights of this idyllic life and Sandy was reluctant to have to return to Miami and the daily grind.

On the flight back, Sandy spoke:

"José, this has been the most wonderful week. The weather, the foods, and most of all **the NIGHTS!!** I hate for it to end!"

"Hey, Sweetheart, this was only the beginning of something lasting and growing with each day!"

A fresh brewed cup of strong Cuban Coffee (laced with a shot of brandy) and Sandy sat down to sort through the accumulated e-mails and phone messages awaiting her at **P.I., inc.** Most were requests for help with personal problems, with a couple calls from lawyers seeking her investigating expertise for their clients.

Ignoring or deleting some, Sandy boiled her potential cases down to three two from lawyers referred by Attorney Endicott and one, a personal plea by a victim of identity theft. This one she put at the top of her priority list. Sandy picked up her phone and called the lady's number.

"Hello. This is detective Sandy Sanchez of **P.I., inc.** returning your call," Sandy began, "I understand you've become a victim of an identity thief. I think we should meet and discuss the details. I can then determine if **P.I. inc.** can be of assistance. I prefer we meet here in my office so I can enter your information in my data base as we speak. When's convenient for you?"

"This afternoon would be fine, if it's OK with you?"

"Fine, make it about one then," Sandy replied.

The lady appeared at exactly one, and introduced herself:

"My name is Ann Ramirez and someone is using my name and information to take out loans, open credit card accounts even write checks all in my name!" she announced.

"I've gone to the police but they have no clue who's doing this. The most they've been able to come up with are a half-dozen fuzzy store and bank surveillance camera pictures. Useless in identifying who the woman is in fact the photos seem to be of two or three different women! This leads the police to believe it's not just one culprit, but two or more!"

"Well, Ann," Sandy remarked, "these types of crimes often are the result of a group of criminals working together. They more than likely are highly organized and tech savvy. I have some very sophisticated computer programs that I'll crank up and possibly nail down their MO. If I can establish a pattern, we might be able to 'head them off at the pass'," Sandy tried to assure her. client.

"What I need from you, Ann, are the bills, collection agency letters and anything else pertaining to the ID theft."

"I brought everything with me that I have, which I thought you could possibly use to 'nail' this bunch!" Ann told Sandy.

"Good! Now Ann, you relax and quit worrying, The first thing I'll do is alert the Credit Bureaus to keep me informed of ANY activity on your accounts. If they make a move to hit your finances again, I'll know and step in to stop them in their crooked tracks, and, hopefully, catch them with dirty hands!"

"Sandy, Attorney Endicott told me, if anyone could bust these bastards it'd be YOU! Thanks!"

'Wait 'til I get these guys in custody, before you say thanks, Honey! 'It ain't over 'til the fat lady sings' as the saying goes!"

Four days and no activity by the ID thieves but Sandy has been far from idle! Gathering all the bills and financial records containing the fraudulent transactions, she proceeded to catalog and categorize them.

One thing she found was that almost all the activity was centered in a five mile radius of the Miami suburb of Hialeah.

"That's where I'll concentrate my search, then!" she decided.

Hopping in her 'Spy Mobile', she headed for the location last hit by the crooks. She had obtained, from the local police, still-photo copies of the few surveillance tapes they had, and began showing them around the neighborhood. The photos were of such poor quality that, even after Sandy had enhanced them with Andy's unique programs, they were still too fuzzy to make a positive ID!.

She made her first visit to the convenience store where the thieves had cashed a forged check. The Hispanic clerk, speaking in Spanish, gave her a better description when shown the photos and Sandy was able to narrow down the physical characteristics of at least one of the women suspects.

With a "muchas gracias" she retreated to her 'Spy Mobile' and entered the new data into her facial recognition program on her computer. After some manipulation she was able to bring up the identification of the woman.

The records showed she was a member of a 'gypsy' family wanted in several southern states for various crimes, from counterfeiting to extortion, and even the old 'Three Card Monty' shell game.

"It's obvious they've graduated to ID theft and are victimizing innocent tax-payers with their hard earned cash, now!" Sandy muttered, *"We'll just have to have them rounded up and thrown into the 'can', before they hurt anyone else!"*

Sandy took what she had learned and turned it over to the Hialeah police. They, in turn, called in the US Treasury Department, because of the counterfeiting charges, and the chase was on.!

Back at **P.I., inc.** Sandy wrote up her report and called her client.

"Ann, we got 'the goods' on those ID thieves and the cops and Feds are rounding them up as we speak. There probably won't be much hope you'll get any of you money back, but your credit has been restored and you can relax, now!"

"Sandy, I can't thank you enough! It's been a nightmare I won't soon forget!"

"I might mention, while we're on the ID theft subject someone has come up with a high-tech way of stealing credit card information it's called a 'RFID' scanner that can pull your card information electronically just by passing it near your wallet or purse. The remedy is carrying your cards in a special metal sleeve which blocks the scanner!

"You just might want to pick up one or more of these sleeves to prevent another rip-off artist from getting you in a 'financial pickle', again!

"They only cost a couple of dollars, CHEAP protection!"

NINE

Sandy's case load had been whittled down to a couple of On-line Dating background checks so she quickly cleaned those off her slate, wrote up the reports and filed them away.

"*I could do with some beach time right now,*" she declared, "*I wonder what José is up to. I think I'll give him a call! It's been too long since I enjoyed his lovin' and I'm gettin' sorta 'horney'!*" she chuckled to herself.

"Girl, I've been waiting for your call!" José answered, after picking up on the first ring.

"You can't imagine how I've missed your voice and the feel **of y**our **sweet lovin' bod**!" he teased her.

"**DITTO,**" Sandy agreed, "It's been too long for me, too!"

"I'll pick you up in forty minutes (or <u>less</u>) and we'll have a quicky lunch and any other 'QUICKY' you might desire!."

"I'll be ready and waiting!" Sandy answered breathlessly.

The 'quicky' Lunch had to wait for the other 'QUICKY' because Sandy met José at the door with only her slippers on.

"Angel!!, From what I see before me, you must be as anxious as I to make up for lost time!"

"You can't imagine!" she answered with a sly smirk.

After a thunderous climax it was several minutes before either could stir enough to dress and think about that 'quicky' lunch.

"Well, Gal, now that we've satisfied one appetite I guess we need to take care of the other one," José said with a twinkle in his eyes.

"Well, OK, IF you're sure the primal appetite is well taken care of!"

Sandy replied.

"For the time being! anyway," was his smiling response.

A leisurely lunch at a South Beach sidewalk diner and it was off to the beach for surf-boarding and sun-bathing until the sun was dipping low over the Miami skyline.

"What do you say to going to my place and I'll have my favorite caterer whip up a nice dinner and deliver it? After dinner who knows what might happen?"

"Yeah! **Who knows**!"

On arriving at the penthouse, José directed Sandy to the large bathroom and told her:

"Go ahead and get a shower. There's a robe in the closet you can put on. I'll call in the food order and then I'll take a turn at washing off the salt water and sand."

He emerged from the other bathroom clad in a duplicate chenille robe, belted at the waist and open at the chest, displaying his pecs.

An hour later José's caterer arrived with a serving cart loaded down with delectable food.

"Jeeze, There's enough here to feed an army. You expecting more company?" Sandy asked.

"No. the Chateaubriand and trimmings are for dinner and the Eggs

Benedict are for breakfast!" José replied.

"Hey, you smooth talkin' Cuban, are you implying I'm going to spend the night?"

"I had kinda' hoped you might!" José replied with a raised eyebrow.

"Kinda' sure of yourself, ain't 'cha, Señor?" she scolded.

"Tell me I'm wrong and I'll dive off the roof right now!" he warned.

He needn't have worried. His threat of a high dive was superfluous as Sandy had no intention of leaving this 'love-nest' tonight and maybe not even tomorrow night!

After the sumptuous dinner they relaxed on the pool deck, cuddled together on an upholstered chaise lounge and enjoyed watching the rise of a beautiful full moon.

The night breezes became chilly, so they adjourned to the bedroom.

José untied the sash at Sandy's waist and let her robe slip off her shoulders and fall in a heap on the floor.

As his eyes took in her statuesque beauty she proceeded to untie his belt and his robe joined hers on the bedroom floor.

With their bodies joined from shoulder to thigh, they moved over to the bed and José gently laid her on the silk sheets.

Soft groans announced the joining of their bodies and grew louder as their passion took hold of their senses.

Sandy awoke to a room flooded with the morning sunlight. Turning she noted that the bed was empty on the other side. Then she heard slight noises coming from the kitchen.

Rising, she donned her robe and padded over the luxurious carpet to the kitchen to discover José industriously slaving over the pots and pans preparing the Eggs Benedict.

Along with the eggs he laid out whole wheat-toast slathered in guava jelly and glasses of fresh squeezed OJ. Fresh brewed dark Cuban coffee. topped off the morning menu..

"Good Morning, LOVE!" she greeted him, "What're you trying to do, spoil me?"

"Only a small favor in payment for a **memorable night**!" he returned her greeting.

"My Pleasure, Señor and I **DO MEAN MY PLEASURE!** The night was mind shattering. I'm still weak in the knees!!

"I think last night calls for a day of R&R on the pool deck so we can 'recharge our batteries," he suggested.

A 'recharge' is definitely what I could use today! "Sandy agreed.

TEN

Sandy returned to work and didn't have long to wait for her next client.

She was just taking her first sip of her morning coffee-fix when a middle-aged woman walked in the door.

"Captain Ramos, who owns a yacht charter service down the coast, recommended **P.I. inc.,** as the people to help me with my problem." she informed Sandy.

"If Captain Ramos sent you, then we'll sure do our best to help," Sandy replied, "Let's sit down and you tell me what we can do for you."

"My name is Helen Dorsey. I'm the mother of 19 year-old twin boys, 'Stan' and 'Dan'.

"Stan lives with me but Dan has been crewing on an 80 foot charter yacht operating out of a Coral Gables Marina at least he was, up until a week ago.!

"I have an emergency at home and I urgently need to locate Dan.

"Stan has been diagnosed with a life-threatening kidney desease and needs a kidney transplant. immediately! Due to the boys' unique DNA only Dan is a possible donor!

"What I need you to do for me is **<u>find my son Dan!!</u>**

"The charter boat he was on made a trip to Belize two weeks ago and, on it's return to Coral Gables, it dropped off the radar. No distress call was received so the authorities are listing it only as 'missing at sea'!" Helen sobbed.

"There could be any one of a hundred reasons communications with the ship were lost," Sandy assured her, "so don't lose hope!

"Give me the name of the boat, the Charter company, and the marina she sailed from, and I'll start the ball rolling to locater your son!"

"Thank you so-o-o much, Sandy! Captain Ramos told me you'd turn over every sea-shell and piece of coral to find Dan!"

"I'll let you know when we find him, as I'm sure we will!" Sandy reassured her.

With the provided information in hand, Sandy went to her computer and ran a check on the charter company and individual owners. Everything there seemed to be 'kosher' so she proceeded to check out the Coral Gables Marina personnel and the other members of the ship's crew., No 'red flags' there, either.

"I'd better put out a 'BOLO' on the boat ('Be On The Look Out for) *and spread it around the Gulf and the Caribbean,"* Sandy decided, *"Some other ship or fishing boat might sight* the 'Mary Ellen' (the charter boat's name). *The more eyes looking, the better the odds of finding her."*

Two days searching produced no results until a pilot flying over the eastern gulf spotted a life raft with seven men on board. He radioed the US Coast Guard it's position and remained circling overhead until a Coast Guard 'Albatross' amphibian aircraft arrived on scene to pick up the boaters.

A radio message from the 'Albatross' confirmed they were survivors of The 'Mary Ellen' but did not specifically identify who they were.

Sandy had picked up on the radio broadcast and immediately e-mailed the Miami Coast Guard asking for the names of the survivors of the 'Mary Ellen'.

Due to typical government 'red tape', an answer was slow in coming.

When the e-mail reply did came, Sandy was overjoyed to see the name of her client's son among those rescued.

Sandy didn't let a second pass before she had her client on the phone.

"I've located Dan, safe and sound The ship had hit an uncharted, underwater coral-head and sprung a leak. It took seven hours before the seriousness of the leak was assessed. By this time the bilges were flooded and more water was flowing into the engine room!

"All hands were ordered into the life boat and the yacht quickly disappeared into it's water grave" she reported.

"Their emergency radio was inoperative so they drifted for two days praying for rescue. Except for a mild sunburn, everyone is OK!"

"**THANK GOD!**" was Helen's jubilant cry.

"As soon as the Coast Guard de-briefs the men they'll be released to go home. I've coordinate with the Coast Guard medical to have your son immediately transported to the hospital of your choice. Contact Stan's doctor and you can make all the arrangements with him for the transplant.

'Good luck and God Bless you all."

"And **GOD BLESS YOU, SANDY**. <u>You've saved my son's life</u>!!"

None of the latest calls or e-mails generated any challenging cases so Sandy decided to spend the time surfing and sun bathing to ease the tension she was feeling. Just as she was about to leave the office, the phone rang.

Sandy hesitated answering not wanting to forgo her plan, but curiosity got the better of her.

"This is Sandy of **P.I., inc.,** how can I be of service to you?"

"My name is Randy Luna and I need someone to find my wife. I went to the police for help, but they say it's a 'personal' problem and, since no crime is involved they 'have no jurisdiction'! I contacted a lawyer and he recommended I get you on the case."

"OK why don't you come to my office and we'll examine all the info.

Then we can decide where to go from there."

"Will ten this morning be OK? I'd like to get this taken care of ASAP."

"Ten will be fine. You have my address, do you?" Sandy asked.

"No problem, I'll see you soon!"

Mr. Luna walked into the office promptly at ten and Sandy sat him down and began taking notes.

"This all began about three weeks ago," Randy began," I started getting strange 'hang-up' phone calls and my wife was spending frequent nights 'out with the girls'! She always had an excuse and was evasive when I questioned her actions."

"Do you have anything more than your suspicions that can explain her behavior, Mister Luna?"

"I have copies of several peculiar e-mails that she neglected to delete.

They hint at what sound like meeting arrangements.

"Then, two days ago, she failed to return home from one of her 'nights out with the girls'. I began calling around to some of her girl friends but they 'hadn't seen her in several weeks' or gave me evasive answers!

"I'm convinced she's run off with whoever was making those calls and sending the e-mails," Randy told Sandy, "I want you to find out who this guy is and where they've gone!"

"With the e-mails I should be able to run down their originator and we'll start a 'Where Is?' search for the sender," Sandy assured him, "give me a day or so and I'll get back with you!"

"Thanks, Detective!"

Sandy began her computer manipulations and was able to hack into the server used by the e-mail writer. It only took a few more keystrokes to learn the identity of the man.

"Ahah," she murmured, *"Now we're closing in!"*

With Andy's imaginative computer programs, she commenced a search for the address, photo and other information needed to track down 'Lover Boy'.

With the details learned, Sandy called Randy.

"Sir, I think we've nailed down the name of the guy who's behind the e-mails and phone calls. I've included his ID in my report. She definitely is with him at that address. I don't know what legal action you want to take but that's up to you. As a private investigator I can't ethically get further involved."

"Detective, you've done me a service." Randy replied, "I guess the next thing for me to do is get me a lawyer and dump her!"

"Good luck,!"

Sandy was finalizing her report for her file when the phone interrupted.

It was Randy

"Sandy, I took your report to my lawyer and he said we need more convincing evidence before we file the divorce papers. I have two boys - four and six and I'm seeking custody but my lawyer says we should have all our 'ducks in a row' so the judge will have no alternative but to rule for me.

"Do you suppose you could investigate further and come up with more proof?"

"Mister Luna, I can sure try. We know where our target lives so I'll set up around-the-clock surveillance on his apartment. That's where I'll pick up his trail. It's for sure, your wife is living with him there.

"When we get the two of them together, I'll stay on their tails and, eventually I'll nail them in the 'act'!" Sandy assured Randy..

Sure enough, Misses Luna was 'shacking up' in 'Lover Boy's' apartment.

That was proven on the first day of Randy's watch, as the two of them walked out, arm in arm, heading for the nearby secluded beach.

Sandy took up a position behind a sand-dune close by and set up her video camera where it could catch whatever action the two might engage in.

With the camera's ultra sharp **Zeiss**™ lens_able to record details down to a single hair at one hundred feet.

Sandy knew she wouldn't miss a thing An hour passed without any really intimate connection between the two, except an occasional hug and a kiss.

"Come on you two," Sandy hissed, *"there's no one on the beach for miles! You can do better than that!"*

As if in answer to her admonitions, the two rolled over and shed their brief bathing suits and went into a frenzy of love making **ALL CAUGHT ON CAMERA!**

"Ahah! Gottcha" Sandy chuckled, *"thanks for making this so easy perfect lighting and camera position! This should put the frosting on Mister Luna's cake! and really make the judge sit up and take notice!"*

When Sandy returned to the office she quickly picked up the phone and contacted Randy Luna.

"Mister Luna! I got the evidence you need to prove your wife's adultery.

The video I have leaves **nothing** to the imagination!"

"Detective, I don't know how I'll ever thank you enough! Those two boys mean the world to me and they don't deserve a mother like her!"

"Oh, you can thank me when you receive my bill!" Sandy laughed.

*"That wraps up another case for **P.I., inc.**"* Sandy said as she closed the file and shoved it into the drawer.

ELEVEN

Sandy and José passed their time with days at the beach, surf-boarding or sun bathing, interspersed with an occasional night of passionate 'bed acrobatics'.

P.I., inc., was in a slack state for a few days so they were spending a good share of their time together. Josés' business was also was in a slump, because many of his clients were away on cruises or traveling to Italy, France, the South Seas or other exotic destinations.

When Sandy finally did receive a significant request for her investigative aid, she approached it with enthusiastic relief. The request came from a World War II veteran looking for a Marine buddy he had served with in the battle for Guadalcanal

"Detective we shared the same 'fox-hole' for three days hunkered down trying to stay alive. On the fourth day the Japanese mounted a 'Banzi' attack and we were both wounded, mine more serious than his.. My fox-hole buddy dressed my wounds as best he could under the circumstances. Navy Medics treated our injuries in the field and, as soon as the fighting subsided, we were put on litters and hustled off to the Navy Hospital Ship 'Repose' standing off- shore.

"On the ship we got separated and by the time my wounds were healed enough to be shipped back 'Stateside' we'd lost all contact.

"I don't know if he survived or 'bought the farm'.!

"I've written the Marine Corps and the recruiting station in his home town, but no one could help me locate my 'fox-hole' buddy. His name is (or was) Lance Corporal Jerry Duggan and my name is Private First Class Henry Wolfe.. We were attached to the Third Marine Assault Force, Company 'C'. He came from a small town in Wisconsin. Can you help me?"

"Marine, it would be my pleasure to do what I can to find your friend Jerry.. Fax me all the details you can round up and I'll start the wheels rollin'."

The next morning Sandy received a bundle of letters, photos, military service records and copies of e-mails Henry had sent to various commands and Marine Corps Stations. throughout the U S and the Far East.

Sandy cranked up the computer program Andy had devised, called 'Where Is?', and entered Jerry Duggan's name and pedigree. Several minutes of browsing the inter-net led her only to his 'last known' address.

In desperation she went to a National Registry of Military Obituaries. nothing there either.

By now Sandy was getting desperate!

"He can't have just vanished from the face of the earth!" she told herself. *"I'll just have to keep turning over more rocks!"*

Just when Sandy was about to report her unsuccessful quest to Henry, she received an e-mail from a lady in southern Indiana inquiring if "she was searching for a Jerry Duggan?".

Sandy immediately called the number listed in the e-mail and affirmed the lady's inquiry and listed some of the identifying information in her files.

"Do you know where he is?" Sandy asked.

"I think we have you missing Marine here. A man fitting your ID lives here in our Senior Living Home. He say's he seems to remember some of the details you described."

"My client is very anxious to see him,. Is he able to have visitors?"

Sandy inquired.

"Oh yes.! He lives here in our 'Independent Living' apartments and, when I spoke to him about this a few moments ago, he was overjoyed to get to see his old Marine Buddy.!"

Sandy wasted no time calling her client with the **good news!**

"GOD BLESS YOU, Detective! This was number ONE on my 'Bucket List'! I'll hop the first plane for Indiana! I can't thank you enough. Send me your bill.!"

"NEVER HAPPN" Private, this one's on me! Your service is more than full payment for anything I can do for you! You two enjoy your well-deserved reunion**!!**"

Sandy told José of the case and was brought near tears when she voiced her great satisfaction in being able to assist the two Veterans get back together after sixty plus years..

"We owe them and all the other vets a debt that will never be paid in full," she said.

"You're SO-O-O right, Darlin'!"

After this case Sandy found it hard to concentrate on any pending investigations.

TWELVE

Sandy screened through all the requests, and hit on one from a lawyer representing a recent immigrant from Africa.

Contacting the lawyer she asked for a consultation to learn the problem.

"Detective, if you can come to my office I have all the paperwork laid out, and we can discuss how we need to proceed," he informed Sandy.

Sandy visited Attorney Arthur's office and they sat down for a briefing.

"Here's the situation, my client is a legal immigrant to the US who sought asylum when the Junta ousted her country's President. She's the daughter of the former Vice President and she is under indictment by the Junta for 'action against the new Regime' of the country now named 'Zenda'. She approached the US State Department for protection but they say it's out of their jurisdiction to provide protection for her.

"I've been working with the State Department and other US agencies trying to get the charges dropped and expunged since she is now a legal resident of the US!

"Well, I don't need to tell you how difficult it is dealing with one of those countries.!"

"Don't I know! I'm a born citizen of the US with Costa Rican ancestry, and I've run into all kinds of 'road blocks' when I try to research any of my ancestors. Foreign countries have very confusing laws that are often very unlike ours in the US.

"So, Counselor, how do you suggest we go about clearing this up?"

Sandy asked.

"My first step was to get copies of the charges and the supporting evidence," Attorney said, "I've looked up their laws trying to find how they conflict with ours, and have found some extreme differences. Our extradition laws allow surrender of a 'legal US resident' ONLY under certain 'capital offenses'!

"What I and the State Department have surmised from the charges, she is NOT being charged with a 'Capital Offense' so, as we see it, she is exempt from being extradited. The Ruling Junta in her native country isn't happy with this and have implied that they intend to take 'EXTREME' measure to exact their 'justice'

"We fear this means her life may be in danger and she needs protection!

The people at the State Department say they can't provide a 'body guard' so I'm asking if you can take on that task?" Attorney Arthur inquired.

"I'm free of any conflicting obligations, right now, so count on me. I'll close up my office until this is over, and I'll move in with your client in the morning!" Sandy agreed.

"With any luck we should soon be able to get her hid away using the 'witness protection' system," the lawyer assured Sandy.

Sandy and Nitsa (her charge) were moved to a 'safe house' apartment in West Miami and they settled in for the long haul or until the Government takes over.

Nitsa spoke fair english so they proceeded to get acquainted and soon adjusted to the confined living conditions dictated by the required security of the situation.

Meals were catered and delivered (courtesy of Uncle Sam). The only out side activity was limited to an occasional short walk in broad day light with both ladies covered by hoodys to conceal their faces.

On these walks, Sandy kept a sharp eye out for any suspicious looking characters and her hand tightly clutching her 9-mm Baretta under her garb!.

All went well with no disturbing incidents to mar the peaceful neighborhood. that is, until the fifth day of hiding out

When the caterer arrived with their evening meal the delivery boy was new and Sandy was immediately alert to the change. As well she should be! The boy wheeled the food cart into the room, whisked away the covering cloth and as he lifted the dome covering the 'food' he grabbed for the automatic pistol lying on the plate!

His movement was a split second too slow! Sandy fired three shots before he ever got a grip on the weapon and he sprawled, spread-eagled, over the food cart without a twitch!.

Nitsa was cowering behind the sofa screaming her lungs out!. Sandy retrieved the Uzi pistol from the serving plate, checked the pulse of the body, and finding him already growing cold, turned to Nitsa to try to calm her.

When Nitsa finally got control Sandy picked up the phone and called her US Marshall contact.

"Marshall, this is Detective Sandy Sanchez of **P.I., inc.,** I have a cleanup here and bring transport for our 'package'!"

The Marshall arrived with a four-man team dressed as carpet cleaners and took care of removing the body and 'sanitizing' the apartment.

"I'll take care of the 'package' (Nitsa) from here, Detective," he instructed Sandy, You're in the clear. This was a 'just' shooting so you won't hear anything more about it later. You did a great job and the 'Secretary' will be so informed!"

"Then, that's it Sir? No paperwork or statements to fill out?"

"Yep, that's all taken care of. You're free to go and Thanks!"

Sandy called Lawyer Arthur to report the closing of the case.

"Counselor, this simple 'body guard' job turned into the 'OK Corral'!

The people of her native country played 'hard ball' and I wound up eliminating their assassin with '**Extreme prejudice'!**" Sandy told him, "the US Marshall on the case cleaned up the mess and shooed me home with a clean slate. I just hope this is the last case like this,. I might not always be so lucky!".

When she finished the briefings with the Marshalls she proceeded to complete her report for her client and file away the case in the 'Closed' file

Her adventure left her with several sleepless nights. Although Marine-Trained killing a human no matter the provocation left it's mark on her psyche.

Sandy hesitated telling José about her latest 'dust-up' with the killer. She decided silence was the better way to go. No need giving him cause for worry.,

"What he don't know don't hurt!" She thought, *"but this does call for a few days of R & R before going back to the old routine!"*

In line with that decision, she called José and suggested a day at the beach surfing and sunning.

"Gal, you read my mind!" he said with enthusiasm, "I've been trying to reach you for days but I kept getting your message machine. Where'd you disappear to?"

"Oh, I had an out of town case that kept me busy for a time," she answered, "It came up out of the blue, so I didn't get a chance to let you know I'd be away briefly. Sorry 'bout that, Lover."

"That means you owe me a whole lotta' **making up,** then!' he warned her.

"I fully intend to pay that debt **starting tonight**!" she assured him, "Pick me up in twenty and we'll hit the surf!"

"Can't wait! I'm out the door in five!"

The surf was rolling in with white-caps topping the waves and the two rode them like Gladiators in their chariots. Returning time after time for another go at the mighty waters.

With a few short breaks to catch their wind and sunbathe, they kept it up for hours, and only called a halt when the sun began hiding behind the shore-side condominiums.

They dined at the Brazilian Bar-B-Q and then retired to Josés' roof-top pool, there to watch the colorful sunset.

When the air began to turn chilly the two went inside for quick showers (en tandem!) and wrapping their arms around each other staggered to the comfort of the silk bed sheets.

"This bed is just too big for **<u>one person</u>**," José informed Sandy, "I've been losing a lot of sleep rolling around here, by my lonesome!"

"Well, Señor, let's have a little more action! So, can the small talk!"

Conversation ceased immediately and the two bodies blended into one, to remain that way until the sun, peeping through the drapes, woke them.

When she returned to work, Sandy found her case load was light so she set to the task of sorting out the possibles from the ridiculous. Much of what she found on her computer and in her voice-mail was 'spam', and she immediately deleted them, leaving only three 'BCs' (background checks) and two divorce investigations.

"These should only take a few days to clear up," she murmured to herself, *"I sure need some simple cases after that 'bodyguard' scrape just finished! I don't want to have to draw my Barretta **<u>ever</u>** again!"*

A few hours on her computer took care of the 'BCs' and she turned her attention to the divorces.

She picked up her phone and called one of the lawyers requesting her services.

"I got your voice-mail that came in while I was involved in another case.

Do you still need my help, Counselor?"

"I sure do, Detective, my client needs evidence that her husband is 'foolin' around," he replied, "He's a coach in gymnastics at the local high school, and seems to be spending an inordinate amount of after-hours time 'coaching'. I need you to watch and observe where he goes and with whom."

"OK, Counselor, send me the information and a signed 'Surveillance Contract' and I'll start 'campin' on his tail', first thing in the morning."

"I'll fax it all to you as soon as we hang up," Attorney Magee replied.

Sandy made an inventory of the supplies on the 'Spy Mobile' and topped off the gas tank, in preparation for an extended stay on board.

"Be Prepared! is my motto," she announced, to no one in particular.

A good night's sleep, and she was up and ready as the sun turned the eastern sky to orange and red.

She set out to begin her watch. of the philandering husband's place of residence. Setting the vehicle's GPS to the address, included in the files the lawyer had faxed her, she sat back to follow the instructions from the machine.

As straight as a homing-pigeon the vehicle sailed to the address and delivered Sandy to her destination.

She scouted the address and found a good vantage point on a side street which provided a clear view of the man's front door and the backside of the house.

"Make a move, now, 'Romeo', and I'm going to stick like glue, with my High Def Video catching your every move!"

The first morning of her stake-out began as her target left his home and drove to the high school. Sandy spent the day camped-out in sight of the school and everything seemed normal UNTIL when school let out he did not proceed home, but drove, instead to a motel noted for it's 'by-the-hour' rental policy!

"Now, me Bucko, just who are you meeting here?" Sandy questioned.

Her answer came in the next five minutes, when, a little sports car pulled up and a a shapely young lady went directly to the room the errant husband had rented.

Sandy was capturing all of this on video with her narration filling in the details. With her 500mm lens she was able to get a needle-sharp image of the 'lady's face.

"This should provide perfect identification of the female for use in the client's future litigation!" Sandy declared, *"now, to move in closer and see if I can sneak a peek into what's happening in that room.*

Stealthily moving closer to the motel room Sandy was in luck! The blinds on the back window were damaged and allowed a small crack to expose the activity within.

"Gottcha!" Sandy breathed, *"Now to find out who his bed-partner is!"*

Noting the license plate number of the sports car, Sandy went to her on-board computer and broght up the DMV records web site. this is when Sandy got a shock!

The car was registered to the high school's 16-year old head cheerleader!

Sandy drove to the city library and obtained the latest year-book and, turning to the Cheerleaders' pages found the name listed for the girl in the motel, The accompanying picture confirmed her as the girl in the room.

A quick call to Lawyer McGee and Sandy reported her findings.

"Counselor, sorry to be the bearer of bad news but, I think we have more than a cheating husband here. He's messing around wirh a **juvenile w**hich makes this a felony. I suggest you contact Child Welfare, and turn the evidence over to them for possible prosecution!" Sandy advised.

'I AGREE!" the attorney replied, "I'll let them handle this one. I know my client will be as surprised, and shocked as I am. We need to get this kind of pervert off the streets! Send me your report and all the evidence you've collected. I want to put this 'molester' away now!"

"For sure!" Sandy stated.

Sandy gathered together the video footage and all her notes and had them messenger-delivered to the Attorney's office before returning to her apartment for a shower and some well-earned rest.

"I don't know why all these 'simple' cases have to turn out to be so damn complicated!" she mused.

After a long, rejuvenating sleep, Sandy decided it was time to give José a call. She was in need of company HIS kind of 'company'!

"Lover," he answered on the first ring, "where you been? I get down when I don't hear you voice or feel you body next to me!"

"Same goes for me, too, Sweet One! If you're not too busy, I'll grab my toothbrush and be right over?"

"Right now ain't soon enough!" José complained.

For three days and nights they couldn't get enough of each other. Eating and sleeping was interspersed with erotic bouts of love making. Their bodies became satiated and occasional showers only prepared them for more!

THIRTEEN

After a time Sandy concluded that **P.I., inc.** needed her attention. On returning to the office, she was greeted by numerous contacts requiring her services. One caught her attention as being out of the ordinary and she called the lawyer who was seeking help.

"Detective, Thanks for returning my phone message. I'm Attorney Jacob Fortuna. I have a client, actually two clients, who are attempting to locate a crooked air-conditioning 'repairman' who has taken this retired couple for $7,000 in a 'scam'!.

"They were having trouble with getting their AC to cool their home, so they answered an on-line ad for a 'complete cleaning and upgrade' of their system for $95.00. They have only a small retirement and Social Security income, so, trying to save expensive repair bills quoted by local AC shops, they called on the on-line company.

"Needless to tell you, when the 'service man' went to work on their unit he found several 'parts needing replacement'.! Total cost was **$7,000!**

"The elderly couple didn't question the price and wrote him a check. He promised to return the next day with the 'necessary parts'.

"The next day came no 'repairman'! the second day still no 'repairman'! They called the number listed on the contract the number was 'not in service'! Day three and day four and still no sign of the 'AC repairman'.

They went on-line and found the web site had been pulled!

"That's when they realized they'd been taken and called me! I've had good reports of **P.I., inc.**'s investigative work, so I'm seeking your aid in helping this couple."

"Counselor, I'd be most happy to go to work on this couple's case. Fax me the details and copies if any paperwork you have and I'll jump right on it.

"I'd like nothing better than to hunt this low-life down and put him away so he can't prey on our elderly citizens any more!"

With the information in hand, Sandy went to her computer and, with the aid of Andy's unique programs, began an 'ALIAS' SEARCH'. If the guy had ever used the same name before, Sandy knew she'd pick up his trial.

Her computer disclosed that the culprit was listed in the search data base along with three other pseudonyms (alias's)!

"Now we're getting' somewhere!"

Sandy next checked with the Better Business Bureau and found, under all four alias's and the company names he'd used, he had a whole string of complaints!

She followed up on the most recent and, by phone, interviewed several of the victims In each case the story was the same, he'd pulled the same sort of 'scam' in several southern cities and states!

One thing appeared in common with most cases he had used the name and address of a company in Sarasota, Florida as a reference to set up his fake web page!

"BIG mistake, Buster" Sandy chuckled, *"I've got you in my sights, now!"*

Back to her 'People Search' program and she came up with the scammer's real name and an address!

With this to report, she contacted her attorney/client and laid it out for him.

"I think we have enough here to nail him, Counselor," She announced.

"I sure hope you can get justice for your clients. Preying on the elderly is about as low as you can get, in my book!"

"Detective, with the evidence you've uncovered I'm filing charges with the Florida Attorney General's Office. Under the 'Elder Care Protection Act' he'll spend ten-to-twenty in a cell with plenty of time to **'cool his heels'** thinking back over his days as a 'refrigeration repairman'! **Pun Intended!"**

"Well said, Counselor!" Sandy replied with a laugh.

"While I have your ear, Detective, I'd like to hire your services for another case. This one is a matter of 'Civil Litigation'.

"My client purchased a two-year-old SUV off an independent dealer, and, after only eight days, the motor blew a gasket due to a leaky oil-pan.

"The dealer provided a 'ninety-day money back' warrantee, but claims the fault was the buyer's for failing to replace the oil when it got low!

"We're filing suit for non-performance of the warrantee and I need proof the leak in the oil-pan existed before purchase."

"Counselor, I have a friend who is a state certified auto mechanic and I'll have him examine the car. If the leak is old, he'll be able to spot it. In the meantime, I'll do a thorough background check on the dealer. With my computer I can dig up any shady dealings he might have in his past!"

The BBB had a file on the dealer that covers three typed pages! The size of the record resulted in him receiving the **lowest possible** rating the BBB awards!

"I guess we got his 'number' now to find proof of intent!" Sandy declared.

For this, Sandy had to contact some of the previous complainants.

Interviewing the victims still in the area she found similar problems with faulty or missing equipment Sandy contacted the lawyer and reported her findings.

"Counselor, this bum has so many complaints against him, I don't know how he's stayed in business this long. It's a wonder one of these victims hasn't taken after him with a gun!

"I don't want to tell you your business, but I think this is a good case for a 'class action' suite. There are upwards of two dozen victims in the BBB files!

If that isn't 'CLASS', I'm a three-tailed monkey!"

"Detective, I'm inclined to think you're right. I'm going to amend my suite to seek a Class Action against this shady character. Get me a list of the other complainants the BBB has on file. With that information I'll have all I need to take him to court!"

The phone was ringing when Sandy opened the office door. She picked it up and the caller asked:

"Can I speak to Detective Ireland, please? This is 'Soapy' at the marina bar in Ft. Lauderdale, and I have some news for him."

"I'm sorry but Patrick Ireland has retired and I am now in charge of **P.I., inc.**. My name is Sandy, but may I assist you?"

"Well, when Detective Ireland was here a couple years ago he was checking out an eighty-five foot yacht for a man interesting in buying it. The craft turned out to be stolen and before Detective Ireland could bring in the cops, the 'seller' cast off lines and disappeared during the night."

"Yeah, I remember that case," Sandy responded.

"Last night a boat slipped into a marina down the coast and has all the lines of the missing yacht. The name's been changed but my friend on the dock says he's sure it's the same craft," Soapy reported, "I figured Mr. Ireland might be still interested in following up on the yacht thief."

"P.I., inc., is always interested in tying up loose ends on an unfinished investigation," Sandy told Soapy, "I'll hop over there and take a look-see. Keep an eye on the boat until I get there. Let me know on my cel-phone if it moves!"

"Will do, Detective!"

Sandy hopped into her 'Spy Mobile' and wasted no time getting to the marina where the stolen yacht had been sighted.

Soapy's friend met her at the marina office and pointed out the suspected stolen yacht tied up in a slip at the far end of the dock.

Sandy compared it's silhouette to the picture Patrick had put on her lap- top.

"If that's not the stolen boat," she state, "I'm a cross-eyed baboon!

Let's get Coast Guard over here before they get 'hinkey' and make a run for it and we lose them, again. I want those crooks locked up this time!"

On being notified, the Chief in charge of the local Coast Guard Station dispatched a high-speed 'Skimmer' to the marina to block the slip and prevent any movement by the stolen yacht. This was followed up with a small boarding party of armed sailors charging down the dock and swarming onto the boat.

The six men on board were taken by complete surprise, two were still sound asleep in their bunks.

With properly executed search warrants, the sailors proceeded to go through the boat with a fine-tooth comb, uncovering stacks of fraudulent registry papers for several large yachts. The 'can-of-worms' brought to light a well organized boat-stealing gang which had been working up and down the East Coast!

"Ma'm, with this operation we've been able to solve several thefts of expensive yachts," the Chief told Sandy, "Thanks to you!"

"**P.I., inc.** is always interested in assisting in any way we can. Your quick response to my call prevented these crooks from evading the law again. Thanks to you and your men for that!"

"You'll be happy to know that the evidence we uncovered in our raid enabled us to located and recover four stolen boats two taken from the builder's yard in Annapolis, one each from anchorages in Newport, and Mystic.

"The insurance companies had rewards out for 'arrest and conviction' of the thieves. Since your diligence and investigative efforts were instrumental in bringing down this gang, **P.I., inc.,** and the marina guard, who first sighted the missing yacht, will be splitting a nice little bundle of insurance dough."

"That will put my agency in fine financial condition and I think the watchful marina guard will welcome the reward for his alertness.," Sandy stated.

Sandy called 'Soapy' and reported the successful apprehension of the yacht thieves.

"I'm sending you a 20% finder's fee for putting me onto this, 'Soapy," Sandy informed him, "It took a couple years to solve this case but you came through, and the justice system is taking care of those crooks!"

FOURTEEN

Things were very quiet around **P.I., inc.,** and Sandy was spending her warm afternoons at the beach with José, sunning and surfing. Evenings they dined at various sidewalk restaurants and spent pleasant evenings 'clubbing' on South Beach, after which they returned to the penthouse for a night of erotic cuddling lasting long into the night.

José awakened Sandy in the mornings with breakfasts prepared with his own hands, served on the rooftop pool deck while watching the sunrise reflected off the glass facades on Miami's high-rises along the Inland Waterway.

Sandy had spent six days and nights in this manner, but soon realized **P.I., inc.,** needed her attention, so she returned to the office to check her e-mails and phone messages.

Surprisingly there were only three requests for help. She read through them and ascertained that two were routine back ground checks for on-line dating applicants which she disposed of in a couple hours.

The third was a text-message from her old time lawyer client, Attorney Endicott.

"Sandy, I need to have you stop over to my office ASAP to discuss a project I have for you. Give me a call and we'll set a time."

Sandy arrived at the lawyer's office and he ushered her into his conference room. Waiting there was a well dressed lady whom Attorney Endicott introduced as 'Mrs. X'.

"My client would prefer not to reveal her real name. Suffice it to say she's a member of Miami's 'higher society' and wishes to stay clear of any scandal this case might disclose," the attorney told Sandy.

"I assure you 'Mrs. X', **P.I., inc.,** has a reputation for using the utmost discretion in these matters. Confidentiality is our watch word!"

"That's good because if any of this leaked out it'd involve many of Miami's elite in life-shattering scandal," Mrs. X replied.

"Now that that's cleared up, Detective," Lawyer Endicott interposed, "here's the situation.

"Mrs. X's father is being 'black-mailed' by a woman who claims he drugged her and then had unwanted sex with her while she was unable to resist. He only remembers meeting her in a hotel bar and having a drink with her.

"The next thing he remembers is waking up, nude in bed and the woman was nowhere around, his watch and wallet were gone

"Two days later he receives a Fed Ex package with some VERY compromising photos enclosed and a crudely printed note stating the pictures were for sale 'to the highest bidder'!"

"I'll need those photos and the note and I'll check with the hotel to see who registered for the room,"

Sandy said, "The registry signature is probably fake, but the handwriting might help in ID'ing whether the woman or someone else wrote it.

"These scams usually involve one or more other participants so we need to approached our investigation with that in mind."

"I have the Fed Ex package, the photos, all the paperwork here along with the statement of the gentleman," the attorney assured Sandy.

"Fine, Counselor, I'll take this all back to my office and see what I can do on my computer and then start from there!"

On the computer, Sandy could only bring up cases with similar MO's (methods of operating) but it gave her a pattern to work from.

She next went to the hotel and, with a couple 'Hamiltons' passed to the manager, she obtained the hotel's surveillance tapes for the night of the incident. From the bar tapes she was able to extract a couple of low-quality shots of the victim and the woman sitting at a table, sipping drinks and, after a few minutes revealed the woman assisting the gentleman from his chair and walking him out of the bar.

"This is going to take a whole lot of 'Photo-shopping' to clean up these images," she told herself, *"I need better images to feed into my facial recognition program. Maybe, with a little luck, I can salvage enough from these tapes to get usable faces!"*

Sandy spent two days at the computer and was eventually able to get what looked like a usable photo of the woman. It took another few hours with the Facial Recognition software before Sandy ascertained that the woman had no previous record so her photo was not on file it was back to 'square one'.

Going back to the tapes she searched back an hour and found the woman in deep conversation with a man.

"This guy just may be the connection. I'll run him through my computer and see what pops up!"

EURECKA! There he was and he had an extensive record, among his most recent, were two arrests for similar scams he'd pulled off in Washington, DC for which he had served six years.

Sandy reported her findings to Attorney Endicott.

"I've pinned down her accomplice, Counselor, but I still haven't connected him to the mystery woman except for their conversation earlier in the hotel bar," Sandy said, "I'm running him through my 'Known Associates' program, now, to see if there's anyone there who fit's the woman in question."

"Good work, Sandy. Keep at it, I know you'll hit pay dirt soon you always do!"

"I won't quit till I nail these two, Counselor!"

In short order the 'Known Associates' program spit out an array of photos of all the women in the man's past and there, number ten on the list, was a snapshot of the woman Sandy was searching for!

Sandy proceeded to her unique programs and fed the record of the man into her 'Where Is ?' search and was soon rewarded with his most recent place of residence.

She cranked up her 'Spy Mobile' and drove to the address and began her surveillance.

"Now, 'Me Bucko', we'll camp here until your whore shows or you take us to her!"

After a few hours of watching, the man exited the door of the motel room and got into a gray sedan and drove off. Sandy debated whether to follow him or wait to see if the woman might be in the room.

She decided to stick with the man and pulled into the traffic a block behind him. Always staying back so as to avoid being spotted, she trailed him to a market where he purchased a sack of groceries and got back into the car.

Apparently he was stocking up for a stay, as he returned to the motel and re-entered the room. He struggled with the door while holding the sack and had to push the door with his foot, in so doing the door stood wide open for an instant and Sandy caught sight of the woman inside.

"AHAAH! This makes it much simpler with the two of you together!" Sandy Said, gleefully.

She continued her observation for the rest of the day and into the night. The 'Spy Mobile' was equipped with a fold out bunk so Sandy packed it in and was awake bright and early in the morning to continue her watch.

There was no activity by noon, so Sandy contacted the lawyer with an update.

"Sandy, my client got another message this morning, from the blackmailer requesting a 'meet' with $100,000 cash to exchange for the pictures." the lawyer informed her.

"OK!, I'll be on his tail when he goes to meet you and we can 'box' him in with the evidence in hand!

"But Counselor, **be careful**, his record shows he's not a stranger <u>to **violence**</u>! He could be 'packin', and we don't want anyone hurt in this party I've had enough gun play to last me a lifetime!"

"Don't worry about me, Detective, I'll be wearin' my vest and my track shoes my motto is 'duck or run'! So, if shootin' starts you'll find me behind the nearest 'dumpster' or leaving a cloud of dust behind me!"

"Be Seein', Ya Soldier!"

The conversation had barely finished before Sandy observed the blackmailer leaving his apartment and climbing into the sedan. In his hand he held a large manila envelope obviously the photographs he hoped to exchange for $Cash$!.

Driving a circuitous route through the city streets, the crook soon pulled over to the curb on the deserted south side of a small urban park.

It was just after dusk and the man sat in his car for several minutes before finally getting out and slowly sauntering over to a bench in the shadow of a large oak tree. He sat down and sat there waiting expectantly.

At this juncture Attorney Endicott strolled up, and, after a few words handed over the envelope with ?cash? in it and accepted the manila envelope from the Blackmailer.

Instantly, they were surrounded by a half-dozen swat team members in full battle gear. The crook was only mildly more surprised at their appearance than was Sandy.

"I sure wasn't expecting all the police presence!" Counselor." Sandy exclaimed as the man was being led away. "I thought this was supposed to be all hush, hush."

"So it is, Sandy, these men are all old friends of mine and sworn to secrecy. I just thought a little insurance wouldn't hurt! As we speak, the gal in the motel is being booked for extortion, so this winds up the 'affair' and no one outside of us is any the wiser!"

"I've had enough excitement for the day, Counselor. I'm heading home for a shower and some sack time," Sandy told the attorney.

"Sandy," the lawyer spoke to her, "you're great at solving crimes and mysteries, but this one is unsolvable:

"A few weeks ago, my wife and three of her lady friends, were on their way home from church after choir practice in preparation for Easter Sunday services two weeks hence. As they drove along the residential street, they met their parish priest riding his bicycle in the direction of the church.

"They tooted their horn and waved and he, in turn, smiled and waved back. For the next few blocks the three ladies chuckled and joked about the appearance of the two-hundred-seventy-five pound priest astride the bicycle.

The poor bike, made of two thin rubber tires and carbon-fiber frame, was badly overloaded. The seat was invisible, being completely enveloped by the portly priest's ponderous posterior.

"As their laughter subsided, they came upon a police road-block. Ahead were two police vehicles, a Fire/Rescue ambulance and a large moving van.

"A patrolman informed the ladies they'd have to wait there until the way was cleared or 'they could back up and detour around the crash scene'.

"The ladies were curious and asked the officer what had happened. and he told them a 'priest on a bicycle had been hit and killed in a collision with the van'.

The women were shocked and asked for a description of the victim.

The policeman's quick description confirmed their worst fears it was their parish priest whom they had greeted down the street just thirty minutes ago.

"It was obvious the person they'd waved to was an apparition of the priest who had just been taken away in the ambulance.

"My wife and her friends have had nightmares of the event for the past several days, naturally.

In the days before Easter two or three more sightings of the bicycling priest were reported but, it was Easter Sunday morning that the church janitor and an alter-boy observed a figure in the white robes of a priest float, as on roller skates, across the floor of the Rectory and pass through a **closed door**!.

"That was the last seen of the 'bicycling priest'!"

"HOLY Mother of Mary!" Sandy exclaimed,

"That's impossible to investigate. It falls under the heading of **'Supernatural'**! I wouldn't attempt to explain the phenomena! Just thinking about it gives me 'goose-bumps'!"

When she told José the story Attorney Endicott had related, his reply was:

"In the rural parts of countries in South America stories like this abound. There's something about the Latin psyche that accepts such supernatural happenings."

"Detective, Attorney Endicott recommended I contact **P.I., inc.,** about a problem a client of mine has that you might help me with." the voice on the phone announced. "My name is Njckoli Doran, Attorney at Law, and my client is the victim of mis-identification and is locked up in County jail charged with robbery of a jewelry store.

"He claims he was on the green playing golf with two brothers at the time the robbery took place. They could vouch for him, but he only knows their <u>first</u> names! Fred and Arthur.

"The jewelry store owner picked him out of a twelve-photo array and two of the store clerks backed up his ID.

"Do you think you can locate those brothers?"

"I can sure try. It might take a couple days, so tell your client to be patient."

"Oh, he won't be going anywhere, the judge has set 'no bond' on him, and he's sittin' in County lockup!" the attorney replied.

Sandy's first stop was the 'starter' shack at the golf course but, unfortunately, his charts only listed first names and start times.

"Did they pay with credit cards?" Sandy asked.

"Yeah, they each used American Express™," he answered, "but the receipts are all kept in the main office."

When Sandy approached the manager in the administration office, he was reluctant to show her the records. But when she explained why a regular customer needed the information, he brought out a file box with dozens of receipts thrown haphazardly together.

"After we've collected on these we only keep the receipts around for a couple months. You're lucky we still have them. Sit down at that table and do your search, and good luck!".

It took Sandy an hour and forty-five minutes to come up with receipts for the day in question showing the full names of the two golfers.

Back in the office, Sandy sat down at her computer and started her 'people search'.

When their names popped on the screen along with addresses and phone numbers, Sandy picked up her phone and reported her findings to Attorney Doran.

"Detective, you've come through just as Bob Endicott said you would.

I'll take it from here and contact the brothers about testifying at my client's Court Hearing.

"Meanwhile please stay on the case and see if you can discover who the 'look-alike' real jewel thief is. There's a five thousand dollar **reward o**ut for him and that, along with your fee from me, should sweeten the kitty quite nicely! Hah!"

"Sounds like a plan to me,!" Sandy laughed.

Using the photo of lawyer Doran's client, she downloaded it into her Facial Recognition software and brought up three subjects baring strong similarities to the client. A process of elimination (age, location, etc.,) centered on one man! Two of the men lived too far out of state to be possibly connected with the robbery, One of those two was even a guest of a Newark lock up at the time the robbery took place scratch him!

The third man fit the profile perfectly, so Sandy reported this info to the Police for action.

He was picked up in a local motel and found still holding some of the stolen jewelry!

"So much for 'eye witness' identifications!" Sandy mused.

P.I., inc.'s workload now centered mostly on on-line dating background checks which Sandy was able to clear in a couple hours each on her computer. However, one request turned up an applicant with a questionable resumé, which Sandy needed to delve into much further before clearing the record.

NCIC listings showed the woman with several past scrapes with law enforcement. They were all adjudicated as misdemeanors and she received probation. Two of her charges, however, were for 'false representation' in a contract dispute which was 'vacated' before any money hand changed hands.

These were enough for Sandy to submit a negative report to the dating web site, and they refused the subject's application.

Sandy decided she'd close up **P.I., inc.,** for the week and spend some time at the beach absorbing sun's rays and loosening up her tense muscles in the warm Atlantic.

FIFTEEN

José called her just before she was closing the office

"Girl, if you can postpone your pending cases, I have a suggestion for a refreshing four or five days."

"My calendar is clear for now. What do you have in mind?"

"One of my lady clients has been bragging about a wonderful spa resort in the Keys," José told her, "I'll crank up the BelAir and we drive down first thing in the morning. We can be there by lunch."

"I'll be ready when you get here!" Sandy enthusiastically replied, "I could really go for a good massage and everything that goes with it!"

"I have a much better idea why don't I pick you up <u>now</u> and you can spend the night at my digs and we'll get an early start?"

"Are you sure you're wanting to 'get an early start' or just a 'late night roll in the hay?"

"I never thought, for a minute, what you're implying!" José said in faked astonishment.

"Why, Señor, what kinda' fool do you take me for?" she laughed.

An early dinner and they repaired to the penthouse and spent a couple of hours in passionate love-making, leaving time for a night of sound sleep before rising and heading for the Keys.

Arriving at Marathon Key before lunch time, they dined on fresh- caught Red Snapper sandwiches at an outdoor beachside café and washed it down with a fine Chardonnay.

After their meal, they found the Spa and took a tour of the facilities.

Everything checked out as Josés' friend had described it. They signed in and were shown to a private pool-side Cabana where they would spend the next four or five days **and NIGHTS!**

Four days of massages, being pounded and mauled, ending in mud baths, and swims in the saltwater pool, occupied their daylight hours. Meals consisting of high protein, low calorie cuisine, were served in their cabana three times a day.

Their nights they spent under the satin sheets snuggled up together after enjoying a session of passionate love-making.

LUXURY.! was the watchword in every phase of the Spa's treatment.

Sandy was overwhelmed by the entire program!

"José, I've been pawed, squeezed and pampered to extreme!" she told him.

"I'm so spoiled! I'm afraid I'll never be able to settle back into my former lifestyle, when I get back to Miami!"

"Well, it's not so far we can't drive, or fly, down here whenever we need to recharge our batteries and I can afford it, if that bothers you!

"I believe: *'The only reason you **make** money is to **spend** money!'*

"***WOW!*** what philosophy," Sandy squealed in amazement.

"Well, Sweetheart, I've been stashing away so much and, I have no one to leave it to when I die. Why let the lawyers slice it all up and spread it around to folks I never hear from, except for some cheap Christmas cards? Half of them can't even remember how to spell my full name!"

"That's sad, but I sure see your reasoning, Lover."

"Before we head back to Miami," José suggested, "I've an idea for a day of adventure to top off this vacation.

"Driving down here I noted a boat rental place just north of here that advertises 'SeaDoos'™ for rent. They're great to sail over the water at about 40 to 50 mph. You'd get a thrill on one of those water motorcycles, Hon."

"Sounds like fun to me," Sandy answered, "I'm up for some excitement after these days of relaxing treatment. Let's give it a spin!"

José signed the rental contract, they parked the BelAir and took off across the gulf waters spewing a 'rooster tail' plume of water behind them.

Sandy clung tightly to Josés' waist and quealed with delight as José guided the craft in a zigzag course around the bridge pilings.

The gulf and Caribbean waters were smooth as glass and the 'SeaDoo' skimmed over the smooth surface effortlessly.

As they proceeded further south on the Caribbean side of the Keys

Sandy called Josés' attention to several red basketball-shaped objects floating on the water's surface.

José slowed down and moved close to one of the objects to inspect it.

"They're probably fishermen's markers but they sure aren't like any I've seen before," he advised Sandy.

Pulling close to one, he reached out to pull it closer and, suddenly a speed boat came racing from the shore, heading directly at them, firing automatic weapons as they approached

"OH, OH!" he exclaimed in alarm, "I know what those balls are, now!

They're floats marking drug drops. Planes fly in low and drop bundles of drugs with those floating balls marking the location of the smuggled 'stuff' for their accomplices on shore to retrieve!"

Before he finished his remarks, he slammed the throttle full open and sped for the bridge, darting among the pilings and heading for a jungle of mangroves on the Gulf side in a effort to evade the pursuing speed boat. It being less maneuverable was slowly losing ground.

It was at this point the men on the speed boat resumed firing at José and Sandy. Spraying the water around the SeaDoo with AK47 bullets.. It was only due to Josés' expert handling, that the SeaDoo finally reached the safety of the inhabited area of the Keys and the boat broke off the chase..

"Grab your cel-phone and call this in to the DEA. and the Coast Guard!" he told Sandy, "Those smugglers are going to be busy trying to retrieve their 'loot' and the Coast Guard needs to beat them to it, and, hopefully catch them in the act.!".

"You said 'this would be exciting' but I didn't think you'd mix me up in a shootin' war!"

"I'm as surprised as you that we ran into that bees' nest, Sweety!"

They went directly to the Coast Guard Station in the Keys and filled out a report of the incident.

"You folks can thank your 'Lucky Stars' that SeaDoo had the speed and maneuverability to outrun the smuggler's boat, Also your handling expertise saved your necks. Congratulations," said the Chief Petty Officer in charge of the Station.

"That's enough R & R to last me for quite a while, Lover, Let's head for home!"

Their brief period of pampering over, and with their lives still intact they returned to Miami feeling refreshed and rejuvenated.

Sandy reluctantly opened up her crowded list of e-mails and listened to her voice mail. She found it hard to concentrate.

All morning her mind kept drifting back to the past four days **and NIGHTS!** It was a mental struggle to keep from picking up the phone and calling José!

She quickly sorted through the communications and boiled the list down to five or six background checks and two messages from Attorney Endicott. These gave no details as to what he needed, but seemed urgent in their wording, so she picked up the phone and gave him a buzz.

"Glad you called me back, Sandy. I have a client who urgently needs your expertise," he said, "He's trying to locate his ex-wife and eleven-year-old son. He was awarded sole-custody of the boy in his divorce case, but three days ago she picked up the boy at school and disappeared from sight.

"The police call it a 'personal' matter so he's on his own finding her.

Will you see if you can dig her out of her hiding place so we can serve the court papers on her?"

"I'll do what I can, Counselor," Sandy replied, "Just fax me all the info and I'll put my electronic 'bloodhound' computer on her trail!" Sandy assured him.

The court records and statement of the husband contained sufficient facts to start Sandy's search-engine steaming down the track. The computer was able to provide Sandy with the woman's history birth place, former residences, employment history, etc. It even brought up the resumé she had submitted at her last job!

"Man, this doesn't leave much to know about her, except WHERE IS SHE?"

Sandy remarked to herself, on reading all the report.

A search of credit card records, utility customer records, new motel registrations turned up no results.

Next step for Sandy was face-to-face interviews with all her friends and acquaintances. Sometimes an un-guarded remark among friends can reveal a clue leading to locating where she might be hiding.

Two of her friends both told of her mentioning the Virgin Islands as a 'beautiful place to live and retire'. A further check of her recent credit card charges turned up an airline ticket purchase. The charge had not cleared before Sandy's previous inquiry, so here was a definite clue for Sandy to pursue.

With some 'finagling' she was able to access the passenger manifest for which the card was used.

There was the woman listed under her maiden-name, 'with son'! She had booked to St. Thomas!

Sandy reported her discovery to Attorney Endicott and asked him whether he wanted her to follow the trail to the Island.

"Detective, I think I can take it from here," he replied, "Now that I know where to find her, I'll fly down there and, with the help of a fellow lawyer I know in St. Thomas, I can serve the papers and force the return of the son.

"Which is all my client really wants. He said he's not interested in filing any kidnapping charges against his ex!

"Thanks for another well-done job, Sandy."

SIXTEEN

Sandy contemplated the events of the past few months:

"I'm quickly realizing that many of my 'simple' cases wind up with having to call in the local 'gendarmes' or the Feds or with having to engage in using firepower which I abhor!

"I'm thinking I should stick to just doing background checks no dangerous consequences there and I can hang on to my sanity."

When Sandy discussed her conundrum with José, he voiced his approval.

"I worry all the time about your work being too dangerous. I know you don't always confide in me some of the life-threatening events. This just increases my concern!

"I have a solution lock up **P.I., inc** and marry me and move in here.

This penthouse is way too big for one person. It needs the two of us to make it a 'HOME'!"

"I don't know if I'm quite ready to take that step, just yet," she answered, "Not that I don't love you, but, I've been so independent all my life, I'd have to make such a major change in my life-style. I need some time to wrap my mind around such an extreme move,"

"Well, just close up the agency, temporarily, and move in with me," he suggested, "Give it a 'trial run', so to speak! We're destined for each other and all it will take to 'finalize' it is a firm commitment to our **LOVE!**"

"LOVER, you sure are a **sweet-talker**!" Sandy laughed," Give me a week to wrap up all the lose ends. I have to sub-let my apartment and clear up any cases on the agenda"

Their 'trial run' lasted for a couple weeks until Sandy succumbed to the more permanent status **marriage!**

Sandy became Mrs. Alajandra Maria Sanchez de Torre y **RAMOS! (Ex** Marine **Ex** Private Investigator)

Her days as Miami's premier female Private Investigator ended with her commitment to being the wife of Miami's leading glamour photographer beginning a new phase in her adventures.

With Sandy's departure from **P.I., inc.,** Patrick Ireland resumed control and found two buyers among friends in the Miami retired police officers community.

"I'm confident that **P.I., inc.,** is in good hands and will keep up the record you set," Patrick assured Sandy, "my wishes for a wonderful life go with you, Sandy!"

Printed in the United States
By Bookmasters